**"I'm a pro, honey. I play for big stakes,"
Nick stated arrogantly.**

"What stakes do you propose?" Kim asked.

"You need money. If you win, you get it. If *I* win, you play my game—marrying me tonight."

"I'll take the risk," she answered boldly. It was worth a reckless fling to have His Arrogance admit defeat. She'd never banked on luck, but tonight she felt it oozing from her fingertips.

Nick's large, dark hand stretched out toward her, and Kim settled her smaller hand within his clasp. "Pretty lady, you've got a bet."

As his fingers tightened about hers, a tide of foreboding washed over Kim, a desperate premonition that she was playing a game far more complicated than poker...

GAMBLER'S LADY

CAIT LOGAN

DIAMOND BOOKS, NEW YORK

GAMBLER'S LADY

A Diamond Book / published by arrangement with
the author

PRINTING HISTORY
Second Chance at Love edition / July 1987
Diamond edition / July 1992

ISBN: 1-55773-720-7

Diamond Books are published by The Berkley Publishing Group,
200 Madison Avenue, New York, New York 10016.
The name "DIAMOND" and its logo are trademarks
belonging to Charter Communications, Inc.

PRINTED IN THE UNITED STATES OF AMERICA

10 9 8 7 6 5 4 3 2 1

For my brother, Greg, and his lady love,
Debbie. May all your dreams come true.

CHAPTER ONE

SHE'S JUST WHAT I'm looking for, Nick thought as his gaze traveled over the woman entering his Las Vegas casino office. He stared at the well-dressed blonde as he ordered his bookkeeper to check the total of habitual gamblers' I.O.U.s. Looking as cool and refreshing as the late April desert wind sweeping across Nevada, the blonde gave a definite lift to his dreary Wednesday.

Standing next to—and in sharp contrast to—the casino's brawny bouncer, Fletch Medski, the woman fitted Nick's list of needs perfectly: feminine, classy, and beautifully mature.

Impatient to hear her voice, Nick dismissed the bookkeeper and jabbed at the button on his intercom. "I'm busy," he barked at the casino's receptionist on the other end of the line. "Don't put any calls through. That vampire—my ex-wife, Laura..." he sighed and eased back into his custom-made desk chair, continuing to study the woman who stood before him. He guessed her age to be in the mid-twenties. "Laura has a nasty habit of calling everything a life-or-death emergency to get through to me. Don't fall for it." He clicked the intercom off with another abrupt movement, tilted the chair back slightly, and crossed his arms comfortably across his chest.

Under his steady gaze, the leggy blonde's body slid

1

restlessly, sensuously within her cream-colored linen business suit. A long string of pearls shifted over her off-white patterned blouse. Clutching her purse, she looked mildly uncomfortable, her blue eyes quickly taking in the room's plush red carpeting and heavy teakwood furniture.

"Is this the applicant for the lady bouncer's job, Fletch?" Nick asked quietly, watching her study the patch covering his right eye.

"Yeah, boss," Fletch's voice rumbled as if every punch he'd taken in his boxing career had landed in his voice box. "Kim Reynolds, meet my boss, Nick Santos. He owns this casino."

"I'm happy to meet you, Mr. Santos," Kim said. Her tone was crisp and businesslike. The underlying huskiness snagged at Nick's ragged nerves.

"Kim." He nodded, thinking again how perfectly she would fit into his plans.

Nick remembered the harshness in his voice when he'd spoken to the receptionist. He didn't often justify his actions to others, but there was something about the classy blonde that warranted an explanation.

"My ex-wife, Laura, is on the prowl," he said. "She'll be here next week, and she'd like to prove I'm not providing a decent home for Cherry, our four-year-old daughter. She wants custody, and I'm determined she won't have it. I haven't figured out all the angles yet, but I will." In a tired gesture, he ran his fingers through his curly black hair barely touched with gray.

He felt the raw scraping of his new beard as he ran a palm over his jaw, automatically glancing at Kim Reynolds's smooth cheeks. His stubble would scrape the hell out of her skin if he kissed her, roughing her peaches-and-cream complexion like a teenager's after a Saturday-night necking session. The immediacy of the unbidden thought jarred him. "It's been a damned long day," he said softly, perhaps more in explanation to himself than to the lovely blonde who still stood calmly in front of him, her deep blue eyes revealing nothing.

Kim felt her full mouth tighten. Santos's ex-wife probably had a good basis for seeking child custody. Kim straightened her shoulders, determined not to let Santos's problems affect her. There was plenty of masculine arrogance in the tone of the orders he issued like a dealer passing out a stacked deck.

She returned his stare with a coolness she did not feel. Even seated, Santos was a big man, rugged-looking but neatly dressed—a modern-day pirate, she thought, right down to the chunky gold bracelet circling his broad wrist. Definitely a man her mother would have termed "from the other side of town." He was attractive, just the type, Kim was sure, to make a woman's heart flutter—some *other* woman. Kim herself had never found anything particularly interesting in the brawny, arrogant type. In fact, there was something about Nick Santos that set her senses on edge—the way he looked at her as if he thought she had some kind of . . . potential.

She'd give anything to be out enjoying the April afternoon sunlight instead of standing here being considered for a position as lady bouncer. She frowned as she remembered the newspaper ad: *Vacancy for female bouncer, Ivory Palace. Top pay. Room and board.* The Palace was the nicest club on "Glitter Gulch," Las Vegas's two-block section of flashy casinos.

Her fingers were beginning to ache from their tight grip on her purse. She had saved a substantial amount of the down payment necessary to open her own health club, and her paycheck as a women's physical-fitness teacher supplied biweekly savings. The "top pay" this position offered would cover the remainder of the down payment, satisfying her banker's demands for approving her loan application.

Kim had steeled herself for this interview with Nick Santos, gambler extraordinaire. Nicholas A. Santos possessed a colorful reputation. A ladies' man and a noted gambler, he was also known as an easy mark for bag ladies and derelicts as well as the big charities. He'd even rescued a baby from a burning building.

A patch covered Santos's right eye, but his left eye was black and glittering between soot-colored lashes. A bluish tinge, evidence of a heavy beard, covered his well-defined jaw. His snow-white ruffled shirt and black jacket emphasized his elegant dark Latin coloring. Santos's chest and muscular shoulders stretched the tailored jacket, and the large red carnation tucked in his lapel seemed tiny against the width of his chest. His deep, raspy tone reminded her of the Sonoran desert wind, its force rattling the sagebrush and rearranging the sand dunes. Kim decided that every inch of Nick Santos's body above the desk epitomized what he actually was—a tough Las Vegas casino owner.

Kim lifted her chin slightly. Santos grated on her nerves; he was too blatantly masculine and his scrutiny of her was relentless. He looked like a man who loved to dominate, she speculated. She lowered her lashes, yet continued to study his raw-boned face. It possessed all the tenderness of a Mack truck, and she was willing to bet he held the same chauvinistic views her ex-husband had: that a woman had her place—in bed, in the kitchen, or mothering children.

She had once loved Richard deeply, but playing hostess for the first years of her marriage had left her feeling restless and unfulfilled. As Richard pursued his corporate image at a dead run, leaving little time for their love, the marriage had begun to crack. Their relationship became superficial as Richard flung nonstop accusations at her. *If* she'd be more responsive . . . *If* she'd have children . . . *If* she'd socialize more with his business superiors . . . *If, if, if* . . .

Fletch Medski's large hand cradled Kim's elbow as he leaned toward her. He whispered in her ear. "Nick's had a bad day. He quit smoking, his ex-wife's gonna visit, and some joker from Timbuktu wearing plaid pants and white socks just took the house for a lot of green."

"Sit down, Fletch. You're making me nervous," Santos growled.

More orders, Kim thought derisively when Fletch lumbered to the leather couch and sank down onto it. She wondered fleetingly how an Iowa farm girl would react to a Latin-tempered man who defined women as "broads."

Her hair curled smoothly about her shoulders as Kim adjusted the collar of her silk blouse, then touched her long string of genuine pearls as if they were a talisman.

Nick continued to stare at Kim from beneath his thick black brows. She felt her palms moisten. Iowa chicken hawks stared at field mice with that same piercing concentration before they swooped to capture and devour their prey.

The single black eye roamed Kim's natural blond hair and patrician face, appraising her.

"She looks like some society queen, Fletch. Are you sure you got the right one? The one the showgirls said was teaching women karate?" Nick Santos leaned back farther in his leather chair, placing his large, expensive, and highly polished dress shoes on the paper-cluttered desk. Kim thought he resembled a sheik contemplating a new girl for his harem—*not* the position she intended to fill.

"Yeah, boss," Fletch answered. "I watched her work out before I talked to her."

Santos's eye caught Kim's blue ones. "Move around here, honey," he ordered, indicating a position beside his desk with a large forefinger. "I want to see all of you."

Kim did not like the speculative gleam shooting at her from beneath the incredibly long black lashes. However, she *did* want his signature on a very large-sized check. "All right," she said tightly as she moved around his desk to stand before him.

He continued to stare at her appraisingly. He toyed with a yellow pencil, twirling it nimbly through his large, strong fingers as though it were a miniature baton as his gaze drifted over her lightly tanned face, touching on her full mouth and the slender length of her neck. He studied her squared shoulders, the fashionable dress suit, and the long, golden length of her legs.

Kim began to feel just the smallest touch of anger. Now Santos looked as if he were sizing her up for sequins and feathers for a Flo Ziegfeld musical, instead of considering her as a bouncer for his casino.

"Married?" he asked. His eyelid drifted down to half mast.

"I was," Kim answered as his gaze strolled down her blouse to the fullness of her breasts.

"Boyfriend?" His voice lowered to an intimate rumble.

The question seemed inappropriate and discriminatory to Kim. She dated frequently, not steadily, but her private life was her own—not her future employer's. "Does it matter if I have a boyfriend or not?"

He shrugged, his broad shoulders settling back into the deep upholstery comfortably. "If you get the job, you'll be working with me. I don't want a jealous lover creating a scene in the Palace. Fights are bad for business." He shifted into the chair as if positioning himself for a better view of her body. "Turn around."

For a moment, Kim wondered if the man had actually ordered her as though he owned her. She flashed him a scathing look before remembering how very much she needed Mr. Santos's fat paycheck.

"It's a simple request, pretty lady," he said more softly. The coal-black eye seemed to smolder as it followed the business suit on a downward trek to her hemline. His gaze srolled down her calves to her high-heeled shoes, then back up to her flaxen curls. "Very nice on this side . . . turn around."

Kim heard the sound of her teeth grinding, but she complied. When she turned toward him, she asked lightly, "Is everything all right?"

"You know it is, lady." When Santos stood up, he towered over her five-foot-five frame. In high heels, she barely reached the satin collar of his jacket. "Has Fletch explained the job?"

She didn't like the probing intensity of his gaze. It pierced her blue eyes and flowed over the contours of her mouth, tracing the upper lip that was incongruously fuller than her lower one. When she could find her voice, Kim answered, "Yes. I know that I'll be helping with the difficult women customers."

"Yeah. It's bad for publicity to have guys the size of Fletch and Ross hustle the lady troublemakers outside. I want the problem women moved out of the casino as quietly and as smoothly as possible. Or, if possible, give them what they want. Make them want to come back when they're not as belligerent—or when they've sobered up a little. Got it?"

"I understand. I have a degree in psychology, Mr. Santos."

"Uh-huh," he agreed cryptically. "I guessed you had a degree in something, lady."

"I can do the job," Kim responded stiffly. The college and the psych major degree had been her parents' idea, as they'd dismissed her interest in physical fitness as nonsense. Santos looked as if *he* possessed a degree, too—summa cum laude in arrogance.

His stare touched her chest. "You don't look very strong. Some of these ladies get physical. I've had to pull a few of them off me."

The man certainly thought well of himself, Kim thought. "I teach at a gym, Mr. Santos. Some of my classes are in self-defense."

"Oh?" The tone of the low drawl matched the speculation rising in the jet-black eye. "You expect to be able to handle both jobs?"

Santos was challenging her and Kim felt anger tingling through her. It was a new feeling, and one she didn't like. It affected her like cat's claws on a polished piece of furniture. She hadn't dealt with many characters like Nick Santos in her lifetime. But now, it seemed, she had to.

"Absolutely," she answered, working to keep her tone even. "I understand the casino job would be for the early evening and into the night. I teach day classes."

Santos's deep laugh was short and rough. "Casino players don't know night from day, lady. We do our biggest business from midnight to two or three in the morning. You may have to work longer hours than you expect."

"I can handle it, Mr. Santos." Kim's long nails bit into her palms. She'd struggled and attained financial independence in the five years since her divorce. Experienced at balancing time and a checkbook to achieve her dream, she knew she could manage both jobs.

A muscle moved in his cheek and the triangular black patch caught the indirect lighting.

"Vietnam," Santos explained as her eyes shifted to the leather patch. His fingers stopped toying with the pencil; he raised his right hand to trace the thong securing the patch to his head. He frowned. "It's not the only scar on me, lady." The planes of his face seemed to tighten as he studied her. His smile was cold. "Some women can't stand the thought of disfigurement. You'll be working directly with me. Does the patch bother you?"

Actually, the patch looked as much a natural part of Nick Santos as his rather shaggy, curly black hair. It completed the pirate effect, Kim decided.

"The patch doesn't bother me, Mr. Santos. When do I start work?"

When he stepped closer, she had to lift her head to meet his penetrating gaze. Dark and fit, he bore the scent of expensive lime cologne. The black cummerbund accentuated a lean waist.

"No one said you had the job yet, Goldilocks," he reminded her silkily. The name—spoken in that raspy baritone—made the hair on the nape of her neck stand up. It taunted her intimately, evoking an unwanted image of the Three Bears' beds in the fairy tale. But Santos's bed would be very large and singular.

"How old are you?" he asked.

Kim's eyebrows shot up. She didn't like his black eye probing her face. "Age discrimination, Mr. Santos? I'm perfectly fit—and very well preserved for thirty-five, thank you."

She instantly regretted the slight edge to her voice. He smiled and stated evenly, "As your employer, I have a right to know. Children?"

Next to her ears, the roots of her hair tingled. She had the uncomfortable premonition that Santos was interested in her as a woman. In the few moments she'd known him, he'd been borderline arrogant and rude. She amended the thought: He was out-and-out arrogant. She liked pleasant men, gentlemen. Santos wouldn't know a meaningful relationship with a woman if it ran over him, she thought.

However, as her employer, he did deserve access to certain areas of her life. "No children," she said quietly. Richard had wanted children, she remembered, but as necessary accouterments to their lifestyle, not because he loved them.

"Nearest living relative?" His eyelid almost closed as he studied her pearl earrings and the unruly tendrils cosseting them.

"My father lives in Iowa." Kim's body tensed as it did whenever she thought of her widowed father. He had never recovered from her mother's death. His notes to her were brief, but he always managed to find space to mention Kim's ex-husband. Remarriage to Richard had been her mother's dream, and her father repeated it often.

Above her eye level, the tendons in Santos's tanned neck stood out in relief. "Little girl. Out on your own at last," he said in a low, careful voice. "Where are you staying?"

What did her lodgings have to do with her employment? Kim felt her frown deepen.

Fletch's voice entered the dueling circle Santos had

drawn around her. "I checked her out. She has an apartment."

Kim shot a thanks-but-no-thanks glare at Fletch. Her home wasn't the Hilton, but it was cozy and served her needs.

"If I hire you, I want you living in a suite upstairs. It comes with the job. And I'll make it worthwhile for you to quit your other job. I don't want you turning up for work tired," he drawled. "Any problems with that one?"

"I understand your concern. I'll give my notice later this afternoon." She hesitated, then asked, "Only one question . . . sir. When do I begin?" Kim rather liked the sudden flaring of Santos's single eye when she emphasized *sir* in a tone that placed a mine field between them. Her tone was businesslike and cool, emphasizing the distance between their positions—and Santos clearly didn't like it a bit. She'd struck a tender spot in his arrogance, and the thought warmed her; he deserved a little of his own for calling her "Goldilocks" and "little girl." For what she'd seen of the man, he could dish it out but didn't expect it returned on a platter.

Santos raised one large dark hand to her upper arm. His fingers wrapped about it loosely. There was a tenseness about him, and she sensed the strength of the man. He was testing her reaction to a bad situation. The alert tension in his large body penetrated hers—Kim knew he wanted a specific reaction. He asked, "What would you do if a drunk—"

"Let me demonstrate, Mr. Santos." Normally, Kim would have used tact to avoid a confrontation, but the gambler had insinuated she wouldn't be able to handle a desperate situation. And there was something very physical about Santos.

Applying only half force to her movements, Kim launched her high heel down onto his foot at the same time she applied a thumb lock to his large hand. She released it quickly. The casino owner frowned, grunted once, and stepped back, rubbing his hand. "You're fast, pretty lady. And smart enough not to use full force on your potential boss."

"I hope I didn't hurt you, Mr. Santos," Kim said sweetly.

His grin was slow and approving. Kim wondered how many women had tumbled into his bed at the sight of it. "Nice," he murmured. "Real nice. You've got the job. You start tonight at eight. Make sure you're moved into the suite by then."

The gleam in his eye was definitely approving and speculative. "Don't forget, lady," he warned. "You work only with me. Fletch, help her move. I don't want some dumb ox following her home tonight."

Dressed in a pewter-colored metallic sheath supported by two spaghetti straps tied behind her neck, Kim stood before Santos's suite at eight o'clock that evening. Nick's rooms were located on the second floor of the casino, next door to her own suite. She squared her shoulders, bracing herself for another meeting with her employer. He'd said he wanted to escort her through the casino personally. She took a deep breath before pushing the gilt doorbell.

The heavy door opened slowly. Standing inches below Kim's original gaze was a small girl with huge, curious blue eyes. Her curls almost matched Kim's own blond shade. The little girl's stare seemed much wiser than her years as she appraised Kim's long riotous curls. Her thumb slid into her mouth and she sucked it solemnly. She placed one worn sneaker over the toe of the other one.

"Hello. Is this the Nick Santos residence?" Kim asked more calmly than she felt. Somehow she'd expected to find a tall beautiful showgirl wrapped around Nick, complete with mussed bed in the background.

The small, pale thumb left the little girl's mouth for an instant. "Daddy likes blondes. He says they have more fun. That's why he likes me best." Ownership rang through the girl's voice, establishing her female territory. Apparently Nick Santos was not to be shared.

Kim reeled from the little girl's name for tough Nick Santos—Daddy. Daddies were men with smiles that didn't proclaim big bad wolf and stares that didn't penetrate a woman's clothing. Nick . . . a father in residence? Kim had expected his daughter to be . . . elsewhere. Somehow the loving-care image didn't suit the man.

Without another word, the girl stepped to one side, holding the door handle. "Daddy's in the bathroom," she informed Kim airily. Though the little girl's upper lip bore a milk mustache and her hair badly needed a brushing, she seemed precocious.

Something fluttered about Kim's heart as she thought of her own childhood. She'd felt like an outsider to her parents' love, but she had entertained herself by climbing trees, making ant farms in canning jars, and playing with the barn cat's new litter of kittens. This little girl's environment consisted of a few toys, a view of neon lights, and an arrogant father. Compared to her youth, this child's life seemed empty, and Kim ached for her. "Could you please tell him that Kim is here?"

The little girl took a deep breath that expanded her Hulk Hogan T-shirt and loosened the waistband of her worn jeans. She yelled, "Daddy!" then she turned back to Kim with a shrug. "He shaves and stuff and sometimes doesn't hear me," she explained in the manner of an adult.

"May I come in?" Kim asked, wanting to straighten the girl's tangled hair. She wanted to do more than that, she admitted carefully. She wanted to hold the little girl. She forced a dry swallow down her throat. *It* came back to her now and then—the emptiness remembered from her miscarriage . . . her own little girl. She probably would have had the same curly hair as Santos's daughter. Kim's stomach knotted and she rubbed it with her fingertips. Her own daughter would have been eighteen now.

"Yeah. Come in," the girl said. "Daddy said a blond broad was coming tonight. Guess it's you."

"Broad?" Kim had never to her knowledge been referred to as a broad. "I prefer to be called a lady," she said as gently as she could. After all, it wasn't the child's fault that Santos possessed boorish manners.

"My name's Cherry. I'm four," the little girl offered with the air of a much older child.

Kim debated the girl's precocious manner and decided that anyone in contact with Nick would age quickly.

The suite was decorated in a tan and brown masculine motif, scattered with an assortment of balls and a tricycle. A Raggedy-Ann doll was draped comfortably over the dark brown velvet of a huge armchair. A child's tea set was carefully arranged on a teakwood table before the sumptuous, long modern couch. Cards were arranged between the tiny china plates.

Cherry's huge blue eyes stared up at her, and Kim smiled. "I used to suck my thumb, too. But I held a security blanket in my other hand. A silky blue one."

"You did?"

"Uh-huh. I used it until I held nothing but threads."

The little girl tilted her head and studied Kim. "Did you play jacks, too? My daddy won't play jacks with me. He says it's a woman d—" She struggled with the word and finished, "dominated sport."

Kim thought of the big gambler playing jacks and laughed. "When I was growing up, boys played marbles and traditionally, they aren't very good at jacks. I'll play you a game now, if you want."

Seated on the floor, playing jacks on the coffee table, Kim enjoyed Cherry's antics. Somewhere between twosies and threesies, Cherry touched Kim's hair and said, "You smell good. Broa—ladies," she corrected, "wear perfumes that make my nose itch. Yours doesn't."

Kim smiled, aching to wrap her arms around Cherry. "I'm not wearing perfume, Cherry."

The little girl frowned. "Then I won't either, when I

grow up. I was worried I'd smell so bad that Debbie's
dog wouldn't like me anymore." She hesitated, then
said, "I want my own dog but Daddy says I can't have
one."

"What about getting an aquarium?" Kim suggested.
"Fish and snails are interesting. He might agree to that."

Cherry pouted. "No way. You can't hug a fish. You
can't take him to bed with you. I want a puppy. But
Daddy says they wet on stuff. I'd put diapers on him."

Kim yielded to the impulse to stroke Cherry's round
cheek. "Well, honey, we'll just have to work on the
puppy idea, won't we?" she asked with a smile.

Cherry's eyes widened. "You'd help me change
Daddy's mind? Fletch is afraid too."

"I'm not making promises, Cherry. But trying won't
hurt, will it?"

"What are the odds? I've wanted a kitten or puppy
for a long time. Daddy is stubborn sometimes." Cherry
sighed and rolled her eyes.

Kim threw the jacks and carefully studied the scattered arrangement for a possible foursies as she thought
about Santos's daughter. Cherry had touched something
inside her, and her motherly instinct had leaped at the
chance to champion a four-year-old who knew about
odds-making.

"Good. You're on time. I like that in a woman."
Nick's husky voice skimmed over Kim's bare shoulder
as she stood near the window with his daughter, studying the Las Vegas lights. Cherry had been unable to
concentrate on the jacks game after mentioning the
puppy, and they'd settled into discussing the most suitable breed.

Kim turned to find him lounging against a door-
frame. The droplets clinging to his dark hair indicated
he'd just showered. His white dress shirt was unbuttoned, revealing a mat of black curls over tanned skin.
The tailored slacks emphasized his long legs and trim
hips.

"Good evening, Mr. Santos," Kim managed to say even as the thought flashed through her mind that she'd never met any man as immediately sensuous as the big one before her. Now he looked as if he'd like to fold her close to him, caress her with his large hands. Santos was a disturbing man. She cleared her throat and said, "I'm ready to go to work."

"I won't take a bath unless you watch me, Daddy," threatened Cherry from somewhere in the lower stratosphere. She marched to him and gripped his pants leg. "My daddy always gives me my bath," she informed Kim. "Unless you want to talk to him about . . . something." She winked and silently mouthed, "Puppy."

His dark fingers laced through her jumbled curls. "That's right, little broad. You run your water while I make Miss Reynolds more comfortable. Call me when you're ready to get in the tub."

His gaze followed the girl skipping from the room. "And don't add a whole box of Mr. Bubble this time." Without pausing, he said, "Sit down, Kim."

She remembered her promise to Cherry. "I . . . uh," she faltered as his gaze sharpened, touching her mouth. "Your daughter would like a puppy, Mr. Santos. It seems like a good idea."

Nick stared at her as if he doubted that she possessed a brain. "I've been all through the puppy subject, lady. Cherry understands why she can't have one," he stated curtly.

Kim refused to be intimidated by his tone. She quoted Snoopy. "Happiness is a warm puppy, Mr. Santos. Children need pets. I still think it's a good idea."

He made a noise in his throat that sounded like a blend of a growl and a roar. "No. I'm not in the mood to wipe up puddles. The subject is closed."

Kim traced his grim mouth and decided that Cherry's puppy would have to wait for another day. Now his eyebrows were jammed so closely together, she wondered if dynamite could dislodge them.

"Fine. Perhaps I should go down to the casino and wait for you, Mr. Santos." Kim felt off-balance. For some reason she hadn't put the problems of fatherhood and Nick Santos in the same mental shoe box.

"Huh-uh. I said I wanted to take you down to the casino and I will. Stay put. Plant it on the couch, lady." The flat plane of his hand swept toward the luxuriously padded furniture. His eyebrows lowered as he studied her curves beneath the smooth fabric. "Nice dress. Classy. I like your style."

"Thank you, Mr. Santos." Kim walked to the couch, wishing she'd worn control-top pantyhose instead of the minimum undies the dress required. She could almost feel his gaze stroke her back, smooth the rounded contour of her derrière. She sat as primly as she could. His eye missed nothing of her thigh as the dress's slit parted. For a single eye, she thought, it was a very busy one.

The famous neon billboards of Las Vegas lighted the streets and major clubs beyond the huge glass window. Kim much preferred to study the people roaming in and out of the casinos than the open-shirted man who stood behind a well-stocked bar. He poured a whiskey neat, capped the bottle, and lifted the shot glass toward her. "Drink?"

"No, thank you. I don't drink." Even if she had, Kim didn't intend to share anything that looked even remotely social with Nick. He was just the type to take a mile if she offered him an inch, she thought. She wanted their relationship to remain strictly business.

She clutched her evening bag like a lifeline. The shadows of the room struck the crests of Nick's curls, creating a blue-black halo. In the short time she'd known him, her female antennae sensed that the gambler was more than a little interested in her as a woman. Now his appraising eye traced the smooth bareness of her shoulders, the tiny halter strings tied at her back.

"I like your hair," he said. "Wear it like that when you work. It makes you look less high society and more like the kind of woman who might be found in a casino. My kind of woman."

Kim didn't like his possessive tone or the challenge he seemed to be throwing at her. She shrugged mentally. The dress was a leftover from her marriage, one of the few things she had taken with her. She had walked away with her pride and a small amount of cash, leaving Richard everything else.

"All right, Mr. Santos. I'll wear my hair like this." She had allowed her hair to dry naturally this evening. It was curlier and only needed a good brushing.

"And cut the Mr. Santos crap. I'm Nick, lady. Most people will assume you're my new lady rather than a hired bouncer. Can you handle that?"

Nick Santos's lady. A chill shot up Kim's bare back. She needed the money—she did not need Nick's large shoes under her bed. She stared at him evenly. "I'm not worried about appearances, Mr. . . . Nick. We have a strictly business arrangement."

"No husband, no boyfriend. Life's over at thirty-five, huh? Honey, I'm ten years older than you, and I think my life is just beginning now."

Fine, she thought as she looked at the rows of twinkling street lights and the blazing neon lights of the clubs scrawled across the night sky. Start without me. Kim mentally thumbed through the male advances after her divorce, and decided that Nick remained true to his bold pirate image—his approach lacked subtlety.

Nick was used to having control of situations and she sensed his dislike at being dismissed in favor of the Las Vegas view. The crisp edge in his deep voice proved her theory. "Do you like your suite?"

"It's beautiful. Thank you."

"If you need anything here, just let me know." He moved gracefully toward her. Big, lean, and dark, he eased down on the couch beside her, his eye gleaming. When Kim inched fractionally from him, he chuckled.

"Relax, lady. I'm just waiting for my daughter's high sign. She's probably trying to flush the excess bubbles down the toilet right now. Are you sure you wouldn't like a drink?"

The man made her skin tingle, her stomach growl, and all the womanly softness in her body jump. Of course she wanted something to drink. "Hot tea?"

"From a china cup?" He chuckled again, indicating the miniature tea set. Somehow a length of masculine arm now rested on the back of the couch near her. His eye twinkled almost boyishly. The heat of his finger prowled over her shoulder and down the center of her bare back.

Kim eased from his touch. "This is quite some dress," he continued when she shot him an expression that had effectively halted other men. "It obviously was purchased by a woman with good taste." His fingers slid beneath her long hair to the knot tied at the back of her neck. Before Kim could move from his touch, she felt a tug and her bodice loosened.

"Mr. Santos! What are you doing?" She gripped the sagging strings, one in each hand, as she twisted to face him fully.

He gazed down at her bodice as if he were a good judge of bra sizes, and Kim felt her heartbeat accelerate, warmth flushing her cheeks. The heated gaze moved down the slenderness of her lap to the slit revealing her bare leg. Kim had never been so thoroughly dissected, inch for inch, by a male stare. She felt the blood course through her veins as if she'd just finished a thirty-minute workout without the cool-down exercises. Within the cups of the dress, her breasts suddenly felt heavy. Kim trembled. She did not intend to be Santos's lucky lady.

"Lady, if some drunk had pulled those strings downstairs, we could have had a riot. In the future, tie a tighter knot in any straps you wear. You move like expensive silk and with a body like yours, some character may decide to play a little joke. Got it?"

"Oh, I've got it." Kim struggled with her temper. "But you keep your hands to yourself. Or lose them."

The black brows rose. "Whoa. Surely you don't think you could stop a man my size with your ladies' self-defense methods?" The raw scepticism anchored in Kim's throat, choking her.

"I'd damn well try, mister," Kim stated.

"Good. I like that. I don't want anyone to think that Nick Santos's lady can't handle herself." He grinned. "Now are you going to let me tie those straps properly or are you going downstairs holding all that up by hand?" His eye shifted to her full breasts.

Kim experienced a sheerly primitive urge to box the gambler's ears. But to do so would mean releasing the tiny straps supporting her bodice. She reconsidered. He was only probing, she decided, as he lounged back against the cushions, careless of the broad bare width of his chest and the taut fabric across his well-developed thighs. And he was grinning at her like he'd found a new toy.

No, she decided, Santos wanted a good lady bouncer, and he was teaching her what she needed to know for the job.

At the same time, glancing at the wide, dark hairy chest, she experienced a sudden urge to run her fingertips across it. She swallowed, trying to take the unsettling image in stride. She was an adult woman, after all, experienced sexually, and Nick *did* exude masculinity. Her reaction was normal, she decided, nothing to be concerned about.

"So do you want me to tie your strings or not?" he asked, studying her face closely. "I like that—a minimum of cosmetics," he murmured.

"Daddy!" Cherry called impatiently over the sound of running water.

His eye locked with Kim's. "Well?"

"I can manage, Nick. Thank you."

"Can you really?" he drawled. "We'll see, gambling lady."

CHAPTER TWO

A HALF HOUR later, Nick settled Fletch comfortably before the big-screen television. Cherry, smelling of baby powder and dressed in a white sprigged-cotton nightgown, clambered up onto the bouncer's lap as if he were an overstuffed armchair. Nick marveled not for the first time at his daughter's ability to wrap the giant man around her pudgy little finger.

With a glance at his expensive gold watch, Nick said, "It's eight o'clock. The casino should be getting busy. Fletch, see that you don't let Cherry talk you into betting—you'll lose."

Crossing her arms over her chest, Cherry looked up at her father as she snuggled more comfortably onto Fletch's padded stomach. "But I like to bet with Fletch, Daddy."

"No." Nick knew his daughter was capable of antics Fletch couldn't possibly handle. "You can watch wrestling, but then straight to bed with you. Got that, Fletch?"

"Yeah, boss."

"Did you and Kim talk about my puppy, Daddy?" Cherry asked sweetly. Then she added, "I know we're getting one in the morning, right?"

Nick chuckled, rubbing her head affectionately.

"Kim may be persuasive, little broad. But not this time. Apartments and puppies just don't mix."

The four-year-old's eyebrows drew together. "I knew I shouldn't have laid odds on *her* convincing you. Don't you be late tonight, Daddy." She scowled at Kim. "If he's late, I'll come downstairs. *I'm* the only broad my daddy loves."

Outside his suite, Nick asked, "What did you think of the little broad?" He wanted to hear Kim's low, husky voice. He'd tapped the woman beneath the surface when he'd tugged her straps free, and Kim's eyes had flashed blue fire. He wondered what it would be like to warm himself in her arms. There was no question about it, he decided, beneath her calm, polished exterior, Kim Reynolds was all woman. He found her cool expression and lifted eyebrows—meant, he knew, to place distance between them—enticing and irresistible. Their relationship was definitely going to be . . . interesting.

"Your daughter is very bright, Mr. Santos—Nick."

Nick walked slowly toward the stairway leading down to the casino, and Kim moved beside him, gliding on long, shapely legs like a dancer, her trim hips swaying slightly, intriguingly, beneath her dress. Her cool aura of independence also suggested loneliness, and he sensed a woman who had known pain behind Kim's smooth manner. But what was the source of that hidden pain?

"Look," he began. "If you get into any real trouble tonight, yell. Fletch or Ross can handle anything you can't."

The cool blue eyes regarded him steadily, then lowered to the casino that was already filled to capacity. "I can handle the job, Nick."

"Lady, there are people down there who my male bouncers can't handle. I don't expect you to take on more than they do. Just watch for women causing trouble. One of the guys will handle the men. If you locate a woman who is a problem, try to calm her down, give her what she wants, and get her out the front door happy. If you can't calm her down, hustle her into my office. Let a cage girl, a dealer, or a waitress know you're headed my way, and I'll see what I can do. Got it?"

"Of course, Nick." The confident answer seemed to glide through her glossy, full lips. He didn't like the way her even tone kept him at a distance—as if he were merely someone to endure for a few hours.

"All my women do what I want," he said smoothly, testing her. The blue eyes flashed at him, no longer cool. It was just the reaction he wanted. Kim Reynolds had a temper and, rubbed the wrong way, she reacted with something that reminded him of steam heat.

"I am not one of *your* women," she enunciated slowly. Nick, who, as a gambler, was used to studying character habits, took note of the soft, clear tone. When angered, Kim's voice dropped and she seemed to be choosing her words one by one. He wondered how her laughter would sound.

"I'm an employee, carrying out instructions," she continued. Kim took a deep breath as if to calm herself, and Nick eyed her low neckline. Kim was well endowed. He promised himself he'd see all of her body one day—the long smooth haunches and slightly narrow hips. When she moved, she seemed to glide like a tawny tigress . . .

The image of a naked Kim gliding toward his bed flashed into his head, and, for the first time in many years, Nick felt like a frustrated, highly sexed schoolboy who wanted to impress his girlfriend. The thought grated—he didn't need a woman cluttering up his emotions at his age. "Just make sure you do carry them out," he said more roughly than he'd intended. "I'll be checking in with you periodically. Mill around. Play the tables and the slot machines. Here."

He reached into his slacks pocket and pulled out a money clip filled with hundred-dollar bills. He extracted and handed her three bills. "House money," he explained. "After this, you'll have an account with the cashier." He liked the way her chin lifted as if she resented taking anything from him; most of the women he'd met lately seemed more than happy to take everything they could get.

He watched her slender hands slip the money into her handbag. "If you want a special drink, let one of the waitresses know. If you want hot tea, they'll put it in a special container. China cups and saucers aren't standard glassware for a casino." He longed suddenly to have those slender hands touch him. He stared at her full mouth, imagining its softness opening beneath his. Damn. He *did* feel like a hot-blooded, love-starved teenage boy, his hormones doing double time each time he caught her clean womanly scent wafting up to him.

"I'll return the money to you, Nick," Kim stated, feeling, inexplicably, as if his mouth had just heated hers. Nick was disconcerting. He looked like he knew he held a handful of aces. At her words, he shrugged, and Kim briefly noted the broadness of his shoulders within the expensive tux.

"Cherry's a very pretty little girl, Nick," Kim said lightly, wanting to change the subject quickly. She hadn't liked taking his money but saw no alternative.

The rugged planes of his face seemed to shift into an expressionless mask. "Cherry looks like my ex-wife," he said noncommittally. "You may as well know that my ex-wife, Laura, has had little to do with Cherry. She never wanted her daughter near her—until lately. The joker she married seems to think Cherry would make a nice house pet."

Kim's eyes traced his strong features and surprisingly found no bitterness there. But his expression was too still, and she wondered if she were seeing his professional "poker face." Was he still deeply affected by his ex-wife?

"Cherry's had her dream about Laura as a loving mother thrown back in her face time after time. It was sheer hell seeing that kid trying to love a mother who just couldn't return it," he said.

He stared down at her. "You're wondering, aren't you, how a little girl lives in a casino?" His long mouth curved into a genuine, tender smile. "It's been tough on her, even with sitters and nursery school. And the Palace has had its share of lively moments with Cherry—like the time when she lost her little pet snake and one of the showgirls found it coiled in her bra." He chuckled and for a moment, just a millisecond, Kim found herself warming to him as the girl's father.

"Damn." Nick shoved one hand into his slacks pocket and rubbed his jaw with the other. "My nerves are shot, and I've got a big game tonight. Laura's arriving next week with her new husband to see about custody of Cherry; that's a hard hand to beat."

The gambler's mouth slid into a wry grin that probably would have charmed another woman. "Are you nervous about your first night as a bouncer?"

Kim watched the people milling about on the casino floor below them. Oddly enough, she felt excited rather than nervous. She'd always liked challenges—much to her parents' and Richard's distaste. In fact, since her divorce five years ago, she'd found that competition and personal accomplishments created a natural high for her. Tonight, Nick had opened an exciting new challenge to her—an interesting and profitable job.

She glanced at Nick's eye, veiled by the heavy sweep of his lashes. "Nervous? Of course. But what if I upset one of your wealthy clients?"

His thick black eyebrows lifted. "If you do, I'll hear about it. Then you and I will have a little chat."

Kim felt the curious little chill sweep up her back. The gambler looked as if he'd enjoy a private tête-à-tête with her. She swallowed a dry lump that seemed to be lodged in her throat.

Taking her hand and looping it companionably through the crook of his arm, Nick guided her down the carpeted stairs. "Lady, our relationship is going to be plenty interesting."

* * *

Kim had worked less than an hour when she noticed a large matron disagreeing with a blackjack dealer. The woman thumped the small man with her purse and looked ready to thrash him. Kim eased by the keno table and moved in next to the enraged matron. "Is there a problem?"

"Obviously, honey. This wimp doesn't know how to play blackjack. He should be fired." She lifted her head and scanned the milling crowd. "I want to see the manager. Now."

Kim glanced at the small crowd gathering beside the blackjack table. "I believe I saw him . . ." She spotted Nick's curly black hair just past the shining pate of a man dressed in large plaid. "Over there. Would you like me to take you to him?"

"Damn right! I've played blackjack all my life, and this here creep is trying to tell me that an ace can be counted as a one. In Sweetwater, Idaho, our ladies' circle never uses an ace for anything but an eleven," the woman stated indignantly.

"I see." Obviously, Sweetwater's game rules needed some updating, Kim thought as she smiled. "Let's see what the manager has to say about this. He's an experienced gambler."

Nick in action as a ladies' man was a memorable sight, Kim decided. He asked the woman if she would mind having a drink with him as they discussed the rules of blackjack. "Thank you for bringing this matter to my attention, Kim. I'd like to speak to Ms. . . ." His voice drifted off and he grinned down at the smiling woman. "What is your name, lovely lady?"

"Mabel. Mabel Schwartz," the woman cooed.

"Well, Mabel, let's find a quiet spot and discuss blackjack. I'll give you a few professional pointers." He smiled, and Kim noticed the devastating whiteness of his teeth against the darkness of his skin.

"Will you two excuse me, please?" she asked.

Later, Nick was not such a pleasant sight. A male

customer the size of a water buffalo had backed Kim against a slot machine, his ham-sized hands motioning very close to her breasts.

Nick's long legs were planted, the entire length of his tall body a threatening male arc. His brows lowered and he set his jaw in a rigid line. "Hello, Roberts. Is there a problem, Kim?"

Actually, Kim had already decided that the large aggressive man could be handled smoothly. He was tipsy and amorous, in need of gentle discouragement. And if that didn't work, she'd decided to revert to a neat chop on his rounded stomach. What she didn't need was Nick's interference.

"No problem at all," she said smoothly. She felt just the smallest tug of anger, and it was a sensation she didn't like. Nick had given her a job to do, and at the smallest problem—one she knew she could handle—he appeared with all the aura of an avenging sheik.

"No problem," he repeated, his lips compressing tightly as he glowered down at her. He placed a big hand on Roberts's chest and shoved lightly. "Back off, buddy. She works for me."

Roberts's florid jowls seemed to shimmy. "Ah, gee, Nick. I didn't know she was one of your broads."

Kim had been called that name too many times in one day. "I am not his broad," she stated hotly.

Nick glanced down at her. "Get into my office and stay there," he snapped.

His commanding tone and the inference that she was *anyone's* broad raised the hair on the back of Kim's neck. Nick's possessive behavior was overbearing, and Kim felt her nails score her palms. Before their divorce, Richard had wanted to control her. He hadn't succeeded, and now Nick wanted to order her about like a disobedient child.

"You could say please, Mr. Santos," she managed to say in an even tone.

Nick's black glossy head swiveled from Roberts, his eye widening as it stared down at her. "What?"

Kim smoothed a curl back from her temple with shaking fingertips. Apparently, Mr. Nicholas A. Santos wasn't used to being corrected. "If you want to speak to me privately, Mr. Santos, all you have to do is say, 'Please wait in my office, Miss Reynolds.'"

"Like hell I will. You're an employee, lady. You jump when I tell you to."

Roberts's bulk seemed to fade into the outer perimeter of Kim's and Nick's private battle. Kim raised her chin and lowered her lids. "Then, I quit. I will not be treated with a hop-toad attitude, Mr. Santos. *You* interfered in a situation that I could have handled."

"Lady," Nick warned in a low growl. A vein throbbed at his temple, and his lean cheeks paled. *"Nobody* talks to Nick Santos that way."

"Well, I'm afraid I just did, Mr. Santos. You have my resignation." Kim turned and managed all of one step away from him before a large hand wrapped around her upper arm.

"We're going to discuss this in my office," Nick growled.

Kim stared down at the large dark fingers against her paler flesh. She didn't appreciate intimidation, physical or otherwise. And she didn't intend to be bullied by this man. She wondered how his six feet three inches would look draped across the roulette table. "Remove your hand, Mr. Santos," she stated slowly and evenly. "Or I will remove it for you."

Something flickered in the gambler's angered expression. Nick's hand loosened, then slid from her arm slowly as if he were caressing a length of warm satin. His slow intimate grin stoked Kim's growing anger. "You've got skin like silk, lady," he purred.

"I could have skin like an elephant, Santos, and I *still* wouldn't want you to touch it," Kim erupted.

"Really?" he drawled, too confidently, Kim thought. "Now that's a real challenge."

Kim was furious. She felt her hands tremble and the blood wash beneath her skin, creeping upward from her throat to warm her cheeks. She had reacted to Nick in a purely primitive manner, and it shocked her. "We're both long past playing adolescent games, Mr. Santos. I've just resigned, and you're being difficult. A business arrangement between us absolutely would not work out."

He watched her like a hungry hawk, his hot stare rattling her surface calm, touching some secret core deep within her. At that instant, Kim admitted to herself that she was not in the same sensual league as Nick. Well, he would simply have to play the game without her . . . with some other woman.

"I can't accept your resignation, Kim. Wouldn't you like to have a cup of tea in my office, and we'll discuss the situation?" His voice was the purr of a jungle cat ready to pounce . . . or was it the deep, throaty, lulling sound a lover might make as his hands caressed his mate?

"My office?" he asked, sweeping the plane of his open hand toward the huge carved doors.

Kim felt an odd sensation race through her, her senses quickening, her blood pumping faster. Nick's challenge tantalized her. Rakishly handsome, he probably turned legions of women into warm jelly. For the good of womankind, Nick deserved to hear a firm "no" once in a while.

When the huge thick door had closed with a final click, Kim wondered why she had been so fascinated with the idea of playing with fire—she regretted not leaving the casino immediately. Her knees were shaking when she pivoted toward Nick.

He loosened his tie and flicked open the top buttons of his shirt, reminding Kim of how he'd looked in the apartment—a lethal male, hungry and on the prowl. She took a deep, steadying breath and instantly wished she hadn't; Nick's eye seemed magnetically drawn to her full breasts.

"Sit down," he ordered; then, looking at her face, he corrected himself. "Will you *please* sit down?"

A pleasurable thrill raced through Kim. Maybe Nick could be trained. She eased onto the red upholstery of a chair and straightened her long skirt. "Thank you."

Nick watched the smooth glide of her slender fingers across her thigh. Kim had incredibly long legs . . . It had been years since he'd really wanted a woman. Now he wanted the classy lady with ruffled feathers sitting in front of him. He wanted the tawny tigress lurking inside her.

Nick had grown up in a tough environment where "waste not, want not" was the golden rule, and he sure as hell didn't want to waste the opportunity to explore Kim Reynolds.

"Look," he said as he leaned his hips against his massive teak desk. "I'm sorry. It's been a long day." He sighed and shot her a rueful smile. "You're right; I should have let you handle the situation."

Kim shifted uncomfortably on the chair, and Nick watched the long, lean curves of her body moving beneath the metallic-colored fabric. An intriguing mixture of thoroughbred and athlete, he thought. Whatever this lady was, he had to know more about her.

"Yes, it ha been a long night, and I'm ready to go home," she agreed, running a hand through her curling blond hair. "I accept your apology." She hesitated, then added firmly, "Your daughter wants a puppy. My advice is to get her one."

Nick noted the smooth golden slant of her cheeks and the clarity of her blue eyes as she leveled a look at him. When he'd entered his living-room suite, Kim and Cherry had been standing at the window, their hands joined. Cherry was usually possessive, but she'd warmed to Kim instantly. He'd had the sneaking suspicion then that, united, the two blue-eyed blondes could manipulate the daylights out of him.

"I'll think about the puppy, Kim." He had the sensation that she was looking straight into his heart, and he had to ask the question. "Do I repel you? Does it bother you to look at one eye instead of two?"

Damn, he thought, as her aqua-tinted eyes trailed over the planes of his face and his stomach performed an unscheduled flip-flop. Why? After Laura's reaction to the loss of his eye, it hadn't mattered to him about other women. Why Kim?

Kim met his gaze, frowning. "No, I've told you, it doesn't bother me. Why do you ask?"

The odd tightness was only a fraction of what he'd felt when his wife had first seen the ugly reminders of his pain. He answered Kim's question as evenly as he could. "My ex-wife can't stand the sight of it. But our marriage was over long before I got this.

"We were married twelve years." He scraped his jaw, thinking back . . . "The first two or three were happy enough, I guess. I married her when I was on leave. The damned war was beginning to escalate, and, silly as it seems, I just had to have someone waiting for me at home. To keep part of me sane, you know?"

He glanced at Kim's intent expression and wondered fleetingly why he felt this urge to open up to her. "I was home on leave a few times. Then, when I was discharged, I was too busy working at building a business —gambling—to worry about the marriage. Laura liked the shield of marriage, and her parents supported her extravagances. She dropped in now and then and we had a good time."

Nick noted Kim's eyelids lowering, sheltering the clarity of her eyes, but he was too wrapped up in the story to stop. "About seven years ago, my old chief contacted me for an undercover assignment in Nam. A friend of mine, listed as missing in action, had escaped from a prison camp and was waiting for rescue in a small village. Since I knew that particular part of the country better than anyone else, I was his ticket to freedom."

His throat felt raw as he swallowed hard and continued. "The village where he'd been hiding had been destroyed by the time I arrived, but I spotted John and turned him over to see if he was alive. I should have known better—his body had been booby-trapped. That's how I got this." He tapped the eye patch.

"Laura couldn't handle even our infrequent meetings then. But by that time she'd gone through her inheritance from her dead parents, and I was her meal ticket. I had acquired some property by then and I wasn't in the mood for a messy divorce." He shrugged. "Funny, isn't it, how many empty years can be involved in a relationship? Cherry was the only good thing that came out of our marriage."

He gripped the edge of the desk, watching her intent expression. This lady represented something he'd searched for and missed in Laura. She had a genuine warmth, and he wanted it for himself. "Sorry. That's a long, sad story," he finished wryly. "Would you like something to drink?"

"I think I'd better be going. My employer at the gym might not have hired anyone to replace me yet and I want to be there first thing in the morning to re-apply. Was there anything else we needed to discuss?"

"I've got a business proposal, Kim. I want you to think about it before you answer."

Kim smiled coolly as she reminded herself that any relationship with Nick was bound to be dangerous. "I believe our mutual business adventures are closed, Mr. Santos."

"Cherry needs a lady like you around her, Kim. She's getting a little ragged around the edges—in fact, her sitter said she's turning into a regular little dictator. How would you feel about helping her?"

"There are dance classes for children available at the gym. I'd recommend them..." Kim sidled around Nick's abrupt offer. The less contact with Nick, the better, she thought, though she ached to cuddle his daughter and make the world right for her.

He shrugged. "Great. She can take whatever you think she should." His large hand chafed his jaw. "She likes you. Usually she's very possessive of me around women."

Kim looked at him, a slight frown tightening her brow. She had a premonition that both Santoses were hazardous, and anyone caught between them was headed on a straight road to disaster with no detours.

Nick pushed an intercom button and spoke into it. "Bring me a cup of coffee and..." He lifted an eyebrow toward Kim. When she didn't respond, he ordered, "Hot tea with lemon. Put it in a china cup and saucer for the lady."

"Nick..." Kim warned. She wanted to get out of Nick's office and back to the sanctity of her gym.

His brows lifted. "Hey, you're here for the night anyway. You can't move your things out until morning. Come in," he said when a light knock sounded on the door.

When the waiter had left, Nick poured tea from a small ceramic pot into a painted cup. He handed the saucer to Kim and sipped his coffee. "I need you, lucky lady," he said quietly.

The back of Kim's neck tingled at his low rasp. Her cup rattled against the saucer she balanced in her other hand. "What did you say?"

Nick placed his coffee mug carefully on a stack of papers. "I'm in a situation, Kim—a difficult one. And you may represent the temporary answer to my problem. Drink your tea; you may need it."

Shakily, Kim sipped her tea. Nick leaned forward, bracing his hands on his knees as he stared down at her. "Lady," he said, "the more I think about this idea, the more I like it. In fact, I'd bet on it."

Kim took another sip of tea, squeezed the juice of a lemon quarter into it, and poured the remainder of the tea into her cup. Nick's expression was satisfied and contemplative. She could almost see the imaginary light bulb glowing over his black curls. She didn't like being the object of anyone's plans.

"Just listen," he ordered.

Kim settled back in her chair. She rather liked the

idea of Nick being in a dilemma. To listen might prove
entertaining.

"And how could I make a difference?" She couldn't
prevent a small smile at the knowledge that she
wouldn't help Nick out of a paper bag. But Cherry was
another matter.

"You could marry me."

The words echoed in her head. Marriage to Richard
had begun based on love and turned into disaster. Marriage to Nick would *begin* with disaster. When Kim finally found her breath, she eased to her feet. Carefully
placing the cup and saucer on the desk, she said as
evenly and as firmly as she could, "No, thank you . . .
sir."

"Every woman has her price, Kim. What's yours?"
Nick's graveled voice caused goose bumps to rise all
down her body and she felt the urge to dump the remainder of her tea over his head. He had nerve if not
manners, she thought.

"Marriage is out of the question, Nick."

"Why? You're single. I'm single. No problems
there." He shrugged one broad shoulder. "If we present
a happy family picture, Laura and her new husband will
think twice about going to court to get Cherry. I think
that Laura's dropping in has a lot to do with my daughter's behavior lately. She's started bullying smaller children recently. If things don't change, she promises to be
a real terror. I'm sure it's a child's rebellion against
things she feels she can't control, so she controls what
is available to her."

Kim nodded understandingly.

"You know the marriage and divorce arrangements in
Las Vegas," he continued. "Some people use them like
swinging doors."

Kim took a deep breath and exhaled. "I guess I'm
old-fashioned, Nick. I don't think of marriage as a con-
venience. Surely you can settle the custody in a logical
way—"

"Logical, hell! Laura hasn't any more warmth than

she has brains. She'd gladly traumatize Cherry to suit her own purposes. It's damned difficult." He ran his fingers through his thick hair and rubbed the back of his neck. "Look, we play house for a while, and send Laura back to New York without Cherry. Then we'll get an annulment, and you'll have a bankroll that would choke a horse. What do you say?"

"Play house, Nick?" Kim shivered. She imagined those large hands stroking her body, touching her in the required public display of affection.

"Uh-huh. There's a ten-acre ranchette I've been thinking about buying. For a price, the owner will leave the furnishings and we'll have immediate possession. By the time Laura arrives, we could be the perfect picture of family life."

Life around Nick was an illusion. He arranged lives and real estate to suit his plans—like a deck of cards, skillfully played. He made her uneasy, excited . . . and curious. "Why is marriage necessary, Nick?"

He glowered at her as if she'd missed the fundamental rules of the game. "Laura's not a total idiot. She knows enough to use an investigation service, and I don't intend for them to find one damn flaw."

"I see. But why me? Surely there are a lot of women wanting to play the loving wife for you." The idea flitted around Kim's brain, growing more tantalizing by the second. She had to suppress a giggle. Nick Santos, tough guy, pleading with a stranger to marry him?

"True. I'm not hard up when it comes to women," he answered honestly. 'But I don't think you're the type to steal everything in sight. And I think Cherry could learn from you."

"You could be wrong, Nick," she warned.

"I'm a gambler, lady. I make my living betting on people and their reactions to a certain situation. Like this." He leaned forward, clasped her upper arm, and began to draw her to him.

Kim reacted instantly. She placed her foot near his, and half turned, her back to him as she gripped his wrist. The judo flip over her shoulder was aborted as Nick's other hand clasped her waist. Somehow she was locked to his hard body, her breasts flattened to his steely chest, her arms pinned beneath his.

He folded her closer to the length of his muscular body. He grinned, easing his lower legs between hers to prevent a knifing knee to the groin. "Green Beret," he explained confidently. "We practiced this stuff all the time. But not with such interesting and beautiful opponents. Now what, lucky lady?"

He gazed down at her breasts thrusting against his chest. "I wondered how you would feel against me," he murmured huskily, the harshness in his expression replaced by undiluted sensuality

Kim's heart pounded in her chest. Held against him, she was powerless to defend herself. She was a little afraid of him . . . And of her own body, which seemed to be flowing to meet the hard planes of his.

"I . . . uh." She struggled for the right logic and felt all rational thought fading out of reach. Nick *was* different from other men—he was much too dangerous. The glow escaping his black lashes caressed her upturned face. She felt . . . consumed, as if Nick wanted something she'd never allowed to fully escape her control.

She tried again, her breathing shallow. "You've made your point, Nick. You're bigger and stronger than I am."

"Uh-huh," he drawled. "And hungrier. For the moment." Nick was all male and the hard press of his body against her softer one was raising very womanly sensations within her. His eye darkened into velvet black, the iris mirroring the pale oval of her face. The arrogant planes of his face bore a pleased expression. "You're a beautiful lady, Kim Reynolds," he said in a tone that made funny little electric jolts race down the length of her body.

His mouth was warm and firm, touching hers lightly. *Coming home . . .* the thought lingered, placing all the coldness in Kim's life outside the realm of Nick's strong arms. *Coming home* . . .

Nick's lips caressed hers gently, easing a path over the full contour of her mouth to the left corner. When his mouth settled fully over hers, Kim was unable to move, mesmerized by the desire coursing through her. It had been so long since she'd made love and now all of her female instincts pulled her toward Nick Santos.

"I knew it," he whispered roughly, his breath sweeping across her cheek. "A beautiful, sensual woman . . ." Nick's tongue traced a moist trail across her upper lip, his eye gazing into hers. The tip of his tongue entered her mouth gently, flicking at the delicate tissue of her bottom lip.

Kim's body suddenly felt deliciously heavy, warm, and pliant. The warmth of his big body seeped through her sheath, heating her breasts. She wanted him closer and instinctively adjusted her hips to his, her palms resting lightly on his broad back. Nick's very male outline settled into the juncture of her thighs as his tongue entered her mouth fully.

Vaguely, Kim wondered if the hungry groan she heard had come from her. Nick's mouth lifted, his roughened jaw lightly caressing her cheek. His breath was hot and uneven against her heated skin as he trailed a row of open-mouthed kisses to her ear. He kissed the soft spot beneath her ear, then nuzzled her curly hair. His large thumbs caressed the fine inner skin of her wrists, then his left hand slid behind her head.

"Oh," Kim gasped, her hands flattening, searching, traveling the contours of his powerful back. She wanted to caress him. Her left hand slid to his shoulders, followed the broad line to his neck, and her trembling fingers curled about the muscled width. His hair was crisp, clinging to her seeking fingertips.

His face lowered to the softness of her neck, his mouth warming it.

Kim groaned again, lifting her body to his tasting mouth. His shirt's studs pressed uncomfortably into her chest. Noting her quick frown, Nick looked down at the jade stones against her flesh, and eased away slightly. "Soft. So incredibly soft. My lucky lady," he whispered huskily.

A tiny shard of reality intruded on Kim's desire. What was she doing? Her lips and body responded to him as though she'd known him for ages—as if they were lovers instead of veritable strangers.

"Nick, no." The words seemed torn from her. Heavy lidded, feeling more like she'd been transported into some magical world than like she was standing in Nick's office, pressed against him, Kim said more firmly, "No."

Nick's eyelid lowered and Kim met the glittering eye with an even stare. "You're something, lady. Fire and ice. Enough to keep a man on his toes. I think Laura would buy the idea of you and me as husband and wife. So, what do you say? Will you marry me?"

"Marriage is a lifetime commitment, Nick." Kim managed to answer huskily. "Not a disposable towel."

He shrugged and the silken cloth of his shirt rubbed across Kim's aching breasts. "Some marriages don't last two weeks. You've been married before and so have I. It's nothing more than a business deal in most cases, anyway."

Unhappily, Kim had to admit her past experiences didn't completely disagree with his assessment. "It's difficult to think in . . . this position, Nick. Will you let me go?"

"Okay." Hesitating, he looked at her swollen mouth and she felt him tremble. Then he was as steady as if it hadn't happened. "What about the deal?"

"Why did you kiss me?" she asked shakily.

"I had to see if my . . . handicap was as revolting to you as it was to my ex-wife. If you'd reacted differently—well, call it job-screening, if you want." His eyebrows lifted and he grinned slowly. "You passed the test, Goldilocks."

She thrust her palms against his chest and felt the heavy thudding of his heart. "Let me go, Nick."

"You could say please," he said, reminding her of his earlier offense. When Kim simply glared, speechless, Nick chuckled. "Anything you say, lucky lady."

His arms loosened slowly and Kim stepped back. Before she could invent a suitable, scathing rejection, Nick chuckled again. "Little girl, you look surprised. Don't be—I've got enough experience to serve the both of us." He trailed a forefinger between her brows before she jerked away. "Such a fierce little face. I get the impression you'd like to beat me." He scanned her furious expression intently, his grin easing. "There is one way you could beat me, sweetheart," he offered lightly.

Kim scowled up at him, her fists tightening at her sides. She was frustrated enough, furious enough, to fling herself at him. "Fat chance," she snapped, just able to control her temper. "I'd have as much chance as an ice cube in hell."

His thick eyebrows lifted upward. "My, my, honey. How you do talk. Actually, my suggestion was that we play cards."

His offer stunned her. The man was crazy—first he wanted to marry her, now he wanted to play cards with her? Nick was not a methodical, practical man. He obviously operated strictly on his instincts—his *macho male* instincts. She lowered her lashes, hating the telltale flush warming her cheeks. Nick needed a bashing, one way or another, she thought wildly. He just begged to be taken down a notch.

Longing to wipe the lazy, confident grin off his handsome face, Kim thought back to her friend the dealer's praise at the gym. Just maybe there *was* a possibility of denting Nick's overbearing confidence. In the exchange for her karate lessons, the woman dealer had offered to teach him her skills at cards, and Kim had proved to be an apt student. When she'd balanced her newly acquired expertise against that of the professional gambler and beaten her repeatedly, the dealer had gasped, "Great gopher guts, honey, with that angel face and your skill, you're a ringer!"

Nick couldn't win all the time, could he? She'd love to have his money jingling in her purse.

She traced the new beard covering his well-defined jaw. Good Lord, why not play him? she concluded. If she walked out now without at least trying, it would nag at her conscience. For the first time in her life, she decided to worry about the consequences when they arose.

"Well, Blue Eyes, are you game or not?" he drawled, prompting her. He grinned. "Of course, I can understand if you don't want to play me." Kim's eyes widened to gaze into his sparkling one. The man had all but taunted, "Cluck, cluck—chicken."

She had never experienced the deep need for revenge, but now it tantalized her. She wanted to crush the boyish anticipation written on his dark face, to make him realize he didn't always hold a pat hand. Especially when other people's lives were involved.

She resented his intrusion into her carefully controlled life. She had to play him. It was a matter of honor.

"Count me in, Nick," she said firmly.

CHAPTER THREE

"I DON'T SUPPOSE you have a favorite card game, do you, honey?" Nick asked a moment later. His tone suggested that Kim had never played anything above the level of Old Maid or Go Fish. "The game is your choice. You call it, Kim. And since I'm a pro and you're not, I'll spot you—two out of three games. Tempted?"

The timbre of his deep voice bore a challenge that screamed to be accepted. He reminded her of a swashbuckler boarding a Spanish galleon—he had to be stopped.

"Oh my," Kim sighed wistfully, baiting her hook. "I wish I knew more about cards."

He chuckled and she wondered how he would look when she took his money. He asked, "Rummy? Go Fish? Crazy Eights? I doubt you're up to poker, lady. They probably don't teach that in . . . Iowa, wasn't it?" Nick's eye glittered beneath the length of his lashes and Kim felt the contours of her full mouth tighten. He was too smug, she thought. He'd stirred her sensually and she resented the bold intrusion into her usually controlled emotions.

"Poker?" Kim's fingertips smoothed the material over her thigh as she thought of the dealer who'd praised her skill. "Isn't that a lengthy game?"

Nick laughed outright, tilting his head to look at her as if she were a child. "There are varieties, lady." He shrugged. "Five-card draw would be a quick game for two players. Do you know how to play it?"

She worked on her expression—hesitant, confused—hoping for the perfect effect on Captain Dynamo's confidence. "I think I do..." She stated the game's rules slowly and precisely as if she were trying to remember.

Nick's jaw worked and the thickly lashed eyelid lowered. He stared at her thoughtfully. "Of course, if you're not up to it...?"

"I'd really like to play, Nick," she agreed softly. Kim was pleased with the slow satisfaction spreading across the rugged planes of his face. *Her* satisfaction would come later—as she walked out the casino's door with enough money to complete her loan.

"I'm a pro, honey. I play for big stakes, not toothpicks," Nick stated arrogantly. "What do you say we make it interesting?" He shrugged. "Or we can forget it, altogether."

She felt the opportunity to flatten Nick's inflated ego sliding from her like a soggy noodle going down the sink drain. "What stakes do you propose?" Kim asked.

"Same as before, lady," he stated flatly. "I want to marry you... for Cherry's sake. And you need money. If you win, you get it, without becoming Mrs. Santos. You can walk out of here with a check in your hand tonight—no problems. If *I* win, you play my game—marrying me tonight—and you still get your money after Laura takes off on her broom."

"Let me see if I have this straight, Nick." Kim stepped from him, her trembling fingers curling into the upholstered back of the chair. He'd taken her hook and was running with it like a hungry trout. "If I win, you write me a check." She named the amount she needed to meet the bank's requirement for a down payment. "If you win, I marry you tonight."

Nick's expression became unreadable. "As I said, if

you think the stakes are too high, we can forget it," he drawled.

"Oh, I think the bet is fair. Especially playing for two out of three games. I'll take the risk," she answered boldly, anticipating his expression as he wrote his loser's check. It was worth a reckless fling to have His Arrogance admit defeat. She'd never banked on luck, but tonight she felt it oozing from her fingertips.

Nick's large, dark hand stretched out toward her, and Kim settled her smaller hand within his clasp. His palm was smooth but strong as they sealed the bargain with a handshake. "Pretty lady, you've got a bet."

As his fingers tightened about hers, a tide of foreboding washed over Kim, a desperate premonition that she was playing a game far more complicated than poker.

Nick walked to the desk, stripped off his jacket, and tossed it across the back of a chair. He pulled his tie from his collar and discarded it on top of his jacket. "This is going to be interesting, lucky lady. I don't know when I've wanted to win a game more—" he drawled, "or been more interested in the bet. Sit down at the table."

He nodded toward the green felt table in the corner of the room and extracted a small box from his desk. "Playing for stakes like these, we'll need a fresh deck."

Settling into the upholstery of the chair, Kim noted the lean power of his body as he sauntered toward her. Nick was purely male, and his lovemaking minutes ago had assured her that he'd had more experience than any other man she'd known. He'd been tender and firm . . . and too damned confident.

His lithe movements reminded her of a big cat stalking its prey. The expensive fabric covering his upper thighs was taut, and Kim found herself wondering how his body looked beneath his clothing.

"You're staring." Nick chuckled as he sat down next to her. "Are you wondering what it would have been like if we'd made love?"

Kim refused to be intimidated. "Not at all. You may be very experienced, but you're not my type."

His grin was a blaze of confidence and humor. "You've got guts, gambling lady. I was wondering what you'd look like wearing nothing at all. In my bed."

Kim smiled as coolly as she could, dismissing the slight chill tripping up her backbone. "You'll never know."

"Don't count on it," he said slowly, his eye never leaving hers. Nick ripped open the box seal with his thumbnail, and the cards slithered out in a row as if arranged by his fingers. "Do you want to deal?"

"Certainly." Kim picked up the cards, shuffled them, and placed the deck before Nick. "Do you want to cut them?"

"Uh-uh. Just deal. Suddenly I'm anxious to get married. It's a strange feeling for a man my age."

Kim stared at the dark curly hair, the silver wings at his temples. He was an interesting man, his character filled with different—and, she had to admit, exciting—facets. And he moved on impulse—like this plan to marry her.

"If you win, how would you explain me to your daughter? She's very possessive," Kim reminded him as she dealt him the first card. She continued dealing until they each had five cards, face down on the table. "Nick? Do you want to discard?"

He studied her unhurriedly, ignoring his cards. "My daughter already likes you, lady. I saw her wink at you. You have a cool, gentle way of handling stress that will be good for her. At the same time, I don't think you'd let her rule you." He paused, then said, "You've been wondering, haven't you, why a man my age would have a daughter as young as Cherry?"

"Yes, I have." Kim picked up her cards. She held a straight flush, five clubs in numerical order.

Nick slowly picked up his cards with one hand, spreading them with the pad of his thumb. He glanced at them carelessly. "I'm fine. No discard."

Kim's blue eyes locked with his as she tried to read his stilled expression.

He said, "Cherry's conception was not very romantic, I suppose. We'd both had too much to drink. When Laura discovered she was pregnant, she was furious and started raving about having an abortion. I knew I wanted my baby. Laura settled for an extra chunk of money added onto our divorce settlement. She took off right after Cherry was born. I've never regretted taking Cherry."

He grinned ruefully. "Well, in the first three months, when she had colic, then later, at five or six months, when she started teething, I did wonder a little . . ."

Kim felt an odd, restless feeling, and knew Nick had reached inside her. He kept turning her thoughts, making her *feel* and think of him as an everyday man. One who liked children. A father worried about an overflowing bathtub. Damn him, she thought, trying to stabilize her opinion of him. He's a gambler, a taker, who wears a possessive macho attitude the way some men wear shirts. Someone needed to cut him down to size. "Show your cards, Nick."

Staring at her, his face expressionless, he turned his cards face up on the green felt. His royal flush, five top cards in the diamond suit, beat her hand, a straight flush in clubs. Kim spread her cards on the table, feeling as if she'd just lost a major portion of her life on the wager instead of a short segment of time. Her stomach contracted and she rubbed it. She chewed her bottom lip and met Nick's unreadable gaze. "Dealer loses."

"You've got two more chances, Kim," he reminded her, gathering the cards with one agile swoop of his hand. He shuffled them, filtering her expression through the incredible length of his lashes. "You look shattered, sweetheart," he remarked in a raspy voice that brought the hairs on the nape of her neck upward.

Two more chances. *Did she really have a chance?* Kim began to wonder, staring at the deft movements of his strong, dark hands shuffling the cards. She took a deep breath, flattening her moist palms on the felt, and splayed her trembling fingers. She struggled to recover her earlier confidence. "Are you going to deal?"

Nck's face was grim. "You look awfully pale." He was too close; his large hand quickly cupped her chin, then released it. "You really hate the idea of being around me, don't you? Why?" His expression was savage, his brows drawn together, creases framing his mouth.

Kim felt as though the floor was softening, becoming spongy, and might at any time absorb her. Straightening in her chair, she mentally chastised herself. Why did she seem to lose control whenever Nick Santos got close? And exactly who had taken whose bait?

His crack of laughter held no humor as he dealt five cards face down. "Cheer up. Maybe you'll win this time." He stared down at her and she sensed his dissection of her emotions. "Nervous?"

"I've never been in exactly this position before, Nick. As a matter of fact, I don't know now why I bet anything," she managed to say shakily, half to herself. Oh, Lord. She'd challenged a professional gambler! She'd pounced on his inference that she wasn't up to his ability. Of course, she wasn't! An old adage raced through her brain like a digital readout—*There's one born every minute . . .*

"What made you think you could win?" he asked curiously. "Most professional gamblers wouldn't challenge me."

"You're just too damned confident. You need a little . . . tempering," Kim admitted more steamily than she wanted. "Are we ready to play?"

He grinned lazily, not allowing her to avoid his scrutiny. "Do you think you're woman enough to 'temper' me, lucky lady?"

Kim stared at him, her throat dry. "I wouldn't want to."

She picked up her cards. Three pitiful little fours, a

five of spades and a six of diamonds stared back at her. "I'll take two more. Aren't you going to look at yours?"

His fingers played across the green felt, the broad tips delicately, lightly probing the material. Kim swallowed, watching the neatly clipped fingernails. She remembered his hands stroking her body, caressing . . .

He grinned—a lopsided affair, crammed with a wolfish confidence. "Hell, I guess I'd better. I've been too fascinated watching your face. You read like a new deck, honey. I'd lay odds you've never played any kind of game with a man. You—"

"I don't want an assessment of my relationships from you, Nick Santos!" Kim interrupted hotly.

Oh, Lord, she realized as clearly as the dots on the cards. It was that same primitive anger he'd probed when she'd gambled recklessly, forgetting the possible consequences.

"I'll stand pat, honey."

She discarded, feeling a genuine edge of fear chill her body. Maybe, just maybe . . . Nick dealt her two new cards. Two eights—she had a full house. A passable hand, she thought. Only four other hands could beat it. "Nick?"

The glimmer of hope died as he lounged back in the chair, spreading his cards on the table. This time he had a straight flush—five angry little hearts all in numerical order. They looked like wounds in her flesh. She'd lost two games—there was no need to play a third. He'd won the bet.

Watching her face, Nick crossed his arms. "You look stricken," he growled, frowning. "This situation reminds me of a story I read to Cherry: "Beauty and the Beast." I've never liked snobs."

"I am not a snob," Kim choked. "Nor am I a broad."

"Hell, I know that." His expression darkened, his brows drawing together. Kim felt the tension lodged in the taut muscles of her neck as his gaze swept over her. "You're a hell of a woman, once your iron control slips. A few moments ago, I was pretty close to all that." His eye flicked over her chest before he continued, "It was soft. Smelled good, too."

When Kim finally found her breath, she gasped, "You are just hideous."

He smiled, and Kim trembled. It was a cold, humorless smile. "I've been told that before, lady."

She realized how he'd taken her accusation. With a feeling she'd opened her mouth and inserted a size 12 aerobic shoe, Kim defined her jumbled emotions. "I didn't mean that at all! I just don't like you," she added evenly, carefully.

"I can live with that," he returned just as evenly, reaching toward her. "Your face is very expressive, Goldilocks," he murmured. "You actually shuddered." His dark fingers swept lightly across the fragile line of her collarbone before she could move from his touch. Nick's fingertips were smooth, cool, and they trembled slightly. But the sensation they caused within Kim was the stirring of desire.

There was a dark intensity written in his face, riveting her. Nick wanted her badly. She read it in his taut features, the brightness of his single eye. It had been a long time since she had been desired with such passion. And instinctively she knew he wouldn't try to dominate her as Richard had; Nick would take her soaring to the heights, raising almost violent passion within her.

Kim was shaken to the roots of her cool composure. Never had she experienced such primitive urges, running the gamut from anger to desire. Nick was a catalyst to emotions she'd previously only heard described.

He glanced at her slender fingers, shaking as they wrapped about his broad wrist. One black eyebrow raised. "Careful, lady mine."

"You are just—"

"A beast?" he finished coolly, withdrawing his hand to pick up the deck of cards on the table. He lifted and rolled one broad shoulder, and Kim noted the heavy muscle sliding beneath the silk material. His hands moved skillfully over the cards, playfully arcing them into the air, spreading them on the table before him and turning them in a domino effect. He picked up the deck, bent it slightly, and fanned it from his left hand to his right.

When Kim stared, fascinated by his skill, Nick turned to her, his hands shuffling the cards easily. "Lady, I was hustling on the streets of Detroit before I was ten. I knew how to stack a deck without getting caught at twelve. For years I supported Ma and four other kids by betting. I know an easy mark when I see one. You didn't have a chance. I'd have gotten you one way or the other." The brittle tone in his deep voice frightened Kim. Nick was tough, and for a reason, but she ached for the little boy striving to bring home his winnings.

Nick's rugged face tightened. His lips pressed together. "Nobody's asking for your pity. I made it okay." He flicked a hot, indecent stare at her breasts as if he had X-ray vision. Kim felt her nipples contract and knew they thrust impudently against the metallic fabric. Nick's gaze darkened. "You're the one with problems now, sweetheart. I get the old feeling that your passion surprises you—"

"I'd like to see you in hell, Nick Santos," Kim burst out before she could halt the words. She was so angry she shook, knowing her face bore the heat of her temper.

"Lady, I've already been there. I dream about Nam until I wake up in a pool of my own sweat."

She swallowed what felt like a dry wad of cotton lodged in her throat. His voice, like gravel sliding down a mountainside, scraped her tense nerves. It seemed she'd lost control of her protective reserve, her nerves, and her life—all in the few hours since she had met this gambler.

Trying to remain calm, Kim glowered at him. Nick continued to look on her with all the easy aura of a sheik regarding his new concubine. With an air of fatality, she allowed herself to realize now, without doubt, what had happened. An opportunist, Nick had nettled her, and she'd taken a wild chance. And lost.

Nick shuffled the cards, playing with them as one corner of his mouth seemed to fight a smile. "You know, lady, I've been through a lot in my life, but the past few hours with you have been the most titillating in an awfully long time." He grinned. His gaze lowered to her chest. "Nice pair."

Kim glanced down at her breasts, burgeoning over the bodice of her gown, then glared at him, enraged. "You are the most crude individual I've ever—"

"I know, a regular beast." He shrugged. "I've never claimed to be a gentleman. But I do admit that you bring out a certain amount of devilment in me. It's fascinating how your temper flares so easily. You're a beautiful lady, but, in a rage, I think you're the most gorgeous piece of female I've ever seen."

"Nick," Kim began urgently. "I am not in the mood to play boy-girl games. In fact, both of us are long past that stage." Oh, well, she thought, what difference could *anything* matter now? If he needed a final humility to make him happy, he could have it. She took a deep breath. "Look. I made a mistake when I tried to play you. A momentary lapse of judgment. Will you release me from the wager?"

"Not a chance. I'm in a fix, and I need you to get Laura off my back. You've got the style that could knock her off her..." After a pause, he said, "High horse."

The enormity of her situation swept over Kim, leaving her feeling slightly dazed—as if she were Dorothy just plopped down in the land of Oz. Maybe she just hadn't awakened this morning and this was all a nightmare. She swept her right hand across her forehead in a desperate attempt to clear her thoughts.

Nick's hand reached for her limp left one and lifted it to his lips. Over her palm, he stared down at her. Something that reminded her of compassion moved across his expression. When his lips sought the pad of her thumb, sucking it into his mouth, Kim trembled.

"You're a lonely lady, aren't you?" he asked softly, curving her palm over his cheek and pressing it with his hand. "My livelihood depends on intuition, and I'd stake this casino on the fact that you haven't had the one thing I *did* have as a child—a warm, loving family. Pop died, but our family was one that stuck together when the going got rough."

His insight was devastatingly correct, and Kim felt a suspicious moist heat behind her eyelids. As a child she had competed, exhausting herself for her parents' approval and assurance that they loved her. In her teen years, she had mistaken a boy's sexual need for love, shocking her parents and losing the baby. Now she wondered if her marriage to Richard was based partially on the fact that her parents had so hardily approved of his family—"Good solid people," her father had said. "He'll be good for you."

"Kim?" Nick asked huskily. "What are you thinking? What's wrong?"

She slid her hand from his warm, rough cheek. Right now she wanted to snuggle against Nick's tall, fit body, bury her face against him, and cry her heart out. But instead she said, "I've just lost a lot of pride. I feel like I placed myself on the auction block and was sold to the highest bidder, Nick. I value my freedom . . . my lifestyle—I worked hard for them, and now, suddenly, they're gone. I am to spend an unspecified amount of time co-existing—acting married—with a man who absolutely epitomizes the values I distrust the most! A swaggering lecher, if you will! What could possibly be wrong?"

Nick's thick eyebrows shot upward. "A lecher?" he repeated in a disbelieving drawl. "Lady, where have you been all your life?"

"Places where you haven't been, Nick Santos!" Kim said in a raspy voice, trembling down to her toes.

His expression darkened and became thoughtful. "I

wonder about that . . . What's in your past, honey?" His fingertip trailed over the full contour of her upper lip, then the bottom one. "There's a lot of pain in you. And I'm going to find out what caused it."

"You have no right, Nick—" Kim began.

Bending, his arm swept beneath her legs and he stood, lifting her to his chest. His dark stare stopped her raised hand as he carried her to the couch. "Don't do it, lady," he warned in a growl.

"I'll fight you, Nick," she returned instantly.

"Don't get any weird ideas, sweetheart. I like my women willing," he said softly as he sat on the couch, holding her on his lap. He reached for his jacket and drew it over her, adjusting it about her shoulders carefully as she shivered. "It's called shock, baby. You'll be back to fighting form in a minute, flashing blue fire from those big eyes. Right now, you look more like a child," he murmured, easing a curl back from her face. "A teary-eyed little orphan."

Kim was so full of emotion, she could barely whisper, "Nick—" His body was so warm, cradling her smaller one as his fingers stroked her hair, untangling it. There was a sadness in his face that she knew was just for her. "I'm fine. Really." Her wobbly attempt at a smile failed.

"Uh-huh," he agreed noncommittally. "And I'm the king of Siam. Whatever made you think you could beat a pro at poker, honey?"

The warmth of his body penetrated hers, and Kim relaxed slightly against him. For a lean man, he was padded comfortably. "I've been practicing with a dealer. In exchange for her karate lessons," she admitted.

He chuckled. It was a deep rumbling sound that vibrated against her cheek. "From now on, I'll give the lessons. In a game requiring real skill, Cherry could have taken you with no problems. With her thumb in her mouth. Your face is as readable as the signs on the Strip. Don't ever get in a game where you have to bluff."

His fingers smoothed her forehead and Kim, mesmerized by his touch, suddenly felt very sleepy. It was so nice to rest against him, and feel the solid thud of his heart against her cheek, the lift and fall of his breathing. The enticing feeling of déjà vu warmed her as it had when he'd kissed her . . . *coming home*. He felt so right, so comforting, so familiar. Without knowing why, Kim circled his neck with her arms and felt his strong ones tighten around her. For the moment, she just wanted to be held.

Nick's breathing accelerated momentarily, then slowed. His lips pressed against her temple, and he stirred restlessly. He took a deep, ragged breath and lifted her chin with his fingertip. "I hope you're damned comfortable, because I'm certainly not."

It had been a long day, Kim thought, fighting the weight of her eyelids. "You won the bet. What now, Nick?"

"You recover quickly, don't you, lady mine?" He chuckled, and eased her head to his broad, comfortable shoulder. "I guess we could plan our wedding now. Any preferences as to which chapel?"

Somehow, she had momentarily forgotten the stakes of the bet—marriage to Nick.

She braced her hand against his chest, and clutched his jacket to her chest, pressing her eyes tightly closed. Maybe she was just dreaming and would wake up at any time. "Nick . . ."

"Uh-uh, no backing out now. Where do you want the ceremony?"

Kim felt as flattened as the tone of her voice. "Anywhere is fine. Just let me know."

"I like the Flowers of Love Chapel," he said thoughtfully. "It's large enough for my employees. We'll close down the Palace for an hour or so. The kitchen staff can manage a reception on a moment's notice. And you'll want your friends to come. We'll wind up the night here in my office—"

Kim closed her eyes. Nick was excited; there was a

charged electricity about him, while she felt as directionless as a buoy without mooring in a large, rough sea, being swept relentlessly into a very deep, ominous ocean. "I can hardly wait," she murmured dryly.

"Hell! Neither can I, honey," he agreed enthusiastically. Nick's mouth settled hungrily over hers.

Kim's eyelids flew open and she scrambled from his lap. "You just have to take advantage at every turn, don't you?" she accused, placing her shaking hands at her waist, her legs feeling about as strong as spider webs.

"Uh-huh. Damn right." He grinned, folding his hands behind his neck. He sprawled comfortably, studying her.

"If you think for one moment, Nick Santos, that you've won yourself a bedtime playmate, you can think again," Kim stated heatedly. She narrowed her eyes as his grin widened. "Separate bedrooms, Mr. Santos, and if you had anything else planned, forget it now! I'll play your little game to get you through this custody thing, and that's it!"

"My, my, honey. Would I have anything else planned?" he asked with an innocent lift of one black brow.

"No telling. But if you come waltzing into my bedroom with any devious, deceitful, bed-hopping, macho plans, I'll walk out the door!"

"You're already talking like a wife," he drawled in that deep, humor-laced tone. "So what can I say, but 'yes, dear'?"

Kim frowned, suspicious of his hen-pecked husband tone. She crossed her arms over her chest and demanded, "Tell me about these marriage plans of yours. I want to know just what's expected of me."

He stretched, extending his arms. The movement was lithe, reminding Kim of the earlier hardness of his body against hers. "Simple. You play wifey when we're in public. Pacify any doubts Laura may have . . ."

"What about my job as bouncer?"

Nick's leisurely attitude shifted to tension as he stood. Looking down at her, he drew on his jacket and frowned. "I won't have my wife working. You'll be paid enough for the marriage."

"Nick Santos, you *are* a chauvinist!" Kim exploded. "I took the job, and I'll do it."

He looked uncomfortable, a muscle moving across the ridge of his tanned cheek. He glared down at her, a slight flush rising from his muscular neck to his darkly tinted cheeks. "Everything changed, lucky lady, when you lost the wager," he stated bullishly. "Nick Santos's wife doesn't need to work."

Kim gasped, infuriated at his masculine pride. "And you called me a snob? You've got cage girls, waitresses, dealers, and showgirls running around out there." She pointed toward the office door. "You hired me—"

His head tilted down to hers, his jaw tightening. "And I can fire you."

Kim was so angry she shook. The man was exasperating! Heaven help the woman who got him permanently. She raised her face to his until they glared at each other wordlessly.

"Great. Just great. So fire me," she spoke out, realizing with a start that she had never had one toe-to-toe argument in her entire life—pre-Nick, she corrected. She didn't feel like backing down, despite his obvious anger. Her thumb jerked toward her chest. "I'm marrying you, aren't I? Well, I made an agreement to work the casino as a bouncer, too. And I'm not welshing in either case. What about you?"

His lips pressed together and Kim thought she heard his teeth grind. "I've never welshed on a deal in my life."

"Well, neither have I. I can handle both jobs, Santos. Tough guy." She thumped his chest with her index finger. "Got it?"

"I don't like bossy women, Ms. Reynolds," Nick grumbled roughly after a moment.

The muscle crossing his left cheekbone contracted;

Nick loomed over her as if he couldn't decide what happened next in this scenario. Impulsively, Kim reached out and patted his cheek lightly. "You'll get over it, Santos. Trust me."

An hour and a half later, after Nick had dislodged a city hall clerk from his bed for the legal paperwork, they were married.

The third finger of Kim's left hand now bore an enormous ruby set in gold filigree—a weighty ring as big and bold as her exuberant new husband. Kim, on the other hand, felt once more like a tired Alice in Wonderland—and the Knaves were winning.

At the chapel's reception, when an inebriated football player tried to embrace Kim, Nick's roar swept across the gayly bedecked crowd. "Leave my wife alone!"

He eased through the showgirls' plumes, stalking toward Kim and the brawny, baby-faced football star who held her. "No kissing, Freddie," Nick ordered curtly.

A female impersonator, a smooth-cheeked man with no eyebrows and dressed in a sequined gown, giggled beside Kim.

"Uh, Nick, I was just going to congratulate the bride," Freddie complained. "She looks like she needs someone to—"

"If she needs anything, *I'm* the one to do it, man. She's my wife," Nick warned threateningly. "Hands off."

Kim looked up at the heart-shaped chandelier, and clutched her huge bouquet of pink rosebuds and tiny white flowers. Until she'd met Nick, her life had been structured—upon rising in the morning, she jogged, then taught aerobics. Each day for four and a half years since she'd moved to Las Vegas, she'd done approximately the same thing. When would everything return to normal in the life of Kim R . . . Santos?

Nick's strong arm looped about her waist, and he drew her to him. "Tired, honey?"

She nodded. Of course she was. In fact, she now

knew the true meaning of the phrase "dead on your feet." It was midnight, and she was wearing the same cream business suit she'd worn when she'd first met Nick. A huge spray of mauve orchids pinned to her lapel exemplified her changed lifestyle. Their afternoon first meeting seemed years away. Where was reality?

Nick, in contrast to her wilted condition, seemed to be thriving on the hubbub, acting as happy as a genuine bridegroom. His elegant off-white tuxedo enhanced his dark, handsome looks.

It was all totally disgusting, Kim surmised, looking for a quiet corner in the spectacular crowd of dealers, cage girls, showgirls, strippers, bouncers, chefs in large white hats, and office stenographers. A cluster of bag ladies had dropped into the packed church for free hors d'oeuvres. Guests of the plumbers' convention, holding their golden plungers aloft, eyed the showgirls.

Nick eased her against a wall, and braced his hands beside her head. He smelled the exotic flowers arranged in her hair. "You're a beautiful bride, if an unwilling one, sweetheart."

She forced the huge bouquet of pink roses between his body and hers. "Don't get too carried away, Nick. Remember, it's only for the duration."

"True. But I think I'm going to enjoy every day of it." His head lowered, and the look he flashed at her was sultry. "Are you going to make everyone happy by kissing me, Mrs. Santos?"

She frowned, already feeling the heat of his face warm her flesh. "Not if I can help it!"

His lips touched hers, then lifted slightly. His cheek rested on hers for a moment before he swept her into a Valentino embrace, bending her backward over his arm. He grinned. "Show time."

CHAPTER FOUR

"IF YOU PLAY with my rear one more time, Nick Santos, I won't care who's watching," Kim whispered fiercely into Nick's ear at five o'clock the next morning. Her palm flattened hard against his stubble-covered cheek, jerking his head closer to hers as the crowd celebrating their wedding milled about his office. "And you'll be dealing cards with one hand."

Holding her on his lap, his large expensive shoes braced on the coffee table before him, Nick stilled, listening to her intently. His right hand rested on the jut of her hipbone while his left one held the champagne glass they'd shared. Kim felt as wilted as the orchid spray across her shoulder. She'd been congratulated enough, and squeezed enough. She just wanted sleep. Nick, on the other hand, acted as if he could outlast the impromptu party.

"What's wrong, lucky lady?" he asked innocently, settling comfortably back against the couch and wrapping her in his arms until her head rested on his shoulder.

Kim glared up at him and said through her teeth, "You've used every excuse to . . . to fondle me in front of everyone."

Nick grinned rakishly and Kim hated his freshness. "Hey, we're newlyweds. Isn't a little petting expected?"

"I expect you to keep your hands to yourself," Kim stated hotly, her cheek feeling the pad of muscle slide as Nick shifted her easily in his arms. He was too big and too confident. She scowled up at him. His buoyant mood riled her down to her bones. "You're overacting, Mr. Santos. I feel like a smothered pretzel and my feet hurt." She glanced at the emptied magnums of iced champagne, the plumed showgirls with sequins glued to their nipples, and the changing tide of dealers, cooks, and customers.

And Nick was watching her too closely, she thought, distrusting the gleam in his eye as it traced her frown.

Kim was a beautiful woman, Nick thought, easing her stiff body closer. Right now she reminded him of a sleek, tawny tiger getting geared up for an out-and-out fight. He looked at the brightness of her cerulean blue eyes, the flash of angry fire blazing beneath the long dark brown lashes. There was passionate heat in Kim, despite her cool ladylike handling of the rowdy well-wishers at the reception.

"I'm usually tying the laces of my jogging shoes at this time of the morning, Nick," Kim stated too evenly. "And you've used every opportunity to . . . to kiss me all night," she accused in that same soft dangerous voice. "I'm probably suffering from lip bruise."

Nick chuckled. "Well, how is a new husband supposed to act toward his wife—honey?" Nick couldn't resist the teasing thrust, and felt her body stiffen in his arms. Kim was an enchanting blend of womanly softness and athletic strength and Nick felt himself begin to harden beneath the roundness of her hips.

She tightened, shifting further down his thighs and glaring at him. "You've got busy hands. And arms like a Herculean octopus. You've practically glued me to you all night. Or morning," she corrected with a sigh, glancing wistfully at the dawn beyond the office window.

Her hand slid to his unbuttoned collar and down to the bare chest beneath it. She curled her fingers in the crisp hair covering his flesh and pulled hard enough to make him wince. "Nick. I warn you. I've had enough. I've been awake for a full twenty-four hours, and if you don't call a halt to this . . . this party marathon, I'll walk straight out that door." She smiled.

Nick smoothed a silky curl behind her ear and noted the tightness framing her full mouth. Her skin was like a baby's, heated by her anger. Something intense and hot roamed within Kim's ladylike demeanor, and Nick thought how easily she could heat the cold, lonely corners of his life.

"Santos," she warned, squirming slightly. "Get me out of here."

"Okay, lucky lady. It's your deal," he murmured easily as he stood up with her in his arms. When heads turned toward him, Nick announced, "Party's over. Mrs. Santos wants me all to herself." Grinning, Nick carried her through the crowd toward the office door. "Don't send out any search parties. See you in a couple of days."

Kim was silent as he drove the red Porsche through the quiet city streets. His large hands caressed the steering wheel. He shifted smoothly, enjoying the powerful car and the stormy woman beside him. Hell, life wasn't so bad. In fact, things were definitely looking up.

She glared at him as he pulled onto the highway leading to the ranchette, an isolated patch of cultivated green in the barren sweep of brown desert sand. "You handle this monster as if you love it, Nick," she said tightly.

"I do love it, honey. It's a hell of a piece of machinery."

"Huh," she snorted, her arms crossing over her chest. "I bet you're one of those men who never lets a woman drive if he can help it. Something to do with male ego."

Nick looked at her sharply. He had the premonition that if Kim weren't so tired, she would be dangerous.

"You're in a snit, little girl. When you're rested, we'll discuss the subject. What do you drive?"

"Something that gets good gas mileage and is automatic—a good old American Ford," she snapped as they pulled into the ranchette's garage.

Nick shot the set of her jaw a hard second look. Damn, they'd just gotten married; she wasn't going to prison. She fingered his ruby wedding ring as if it were something he'd found in a box of Cracker Jacks instead of the most expensive jewelry store in Las Vegas. "Is anything wrong, Kim?"

"What could possibly be wrong, Nicholas?" she asked too softly as he opened her car door. She stood and the morning light stroked her long, smooth legs.

"You just don't act like a bride," he grumbled. For some reason he wanted her to be as happy as he felt.

Her stare was long and cool. "Huh. What do you know about that?"

Nick could feel himself heating up. He wasn't *that* bad. In fact, some women considered him pretty eligible. He gritted his teeth and jerked their overnight bags from the back of the car.

Satisfied that Nick was in a snit now, too, Kim studied the meandering hacienda-style ranch house from tiled roof and stuccoed, arched porch to the yucca plants studding the rock-lined walkways. An underground sprinkling system watered the spacious lawn. Slipping her shoes off, she followed Nick's taut back to the house. He unlocked the red carved door.

The empty house loomed before Kim, its shadowy interiors as unwelcoming as her new marriage.

"I know you're going to resent this, but damned if I don't have to do it anyway," Nick said, scooping her into his strong arms. He carried her across the threshold and eased her gently to her feet, his hands sliding reluctantly away.

Kim faced him. "You're right. I didn't like it. Nor did I like being mauled for . . ." She checked her slim gold wristwatch. "Six straight hours. I've got whisker burn all over my face."

Nick's black brows rose. "Mauled, Kim? I was pleasing women while you were learning how to skip rope. But I'll remember to shave next time."

He looked confident that women coveted his touch. Kim's finely shaped eyebrows drew together, the hair on the back of her neck stiffening as would a challenged alley cat's. "Mauled," she said in an irrevocable tone. "And you probably crushed them. You must weigh a ton."

Ignoring Nick's stunned expression, she waved her hand through space toward the sprawling house and asked airily, "Where are we?"

He closed the heavy door with a click that jarred Kim's unsteady bones. He turned on a pottery lamp. "Our new home. I purchased it sometime between marrying you and mauling you."

Kim eyed his stiff back as he walked, carrying their cases, into the sunken living room filled with contemporary furniture and paintings. A huge sectional couch dominated the room, almost forming a square. Large, airy pictures in ochers and siennas covered the white adobe brick walls, and rich white and brown Alpaca rugs covered the wooden-planked floors. Hallways angled from the room, and the rising sun shone pink beyond the patio doors. She wondered vaguely if she were sleeping standing on her feet, when he turned to her impatiently.

"Come on. If you're not interested in seeing the house now, I'll show you the bedroom."

"My bedroom, Nick."

He took a deep sigh that lifted the tuft of black hair curling at the base of his throat. His mouth tightened ominously as he leveled a dark stare at her. "Look. You're dead on your feet, sulking, and you can trust me not to make love to you now. You're not the only one who's had a long day."

Following him, Kim marveled at the space in the

house. He opened a dark, polished door and entered a bedroom where he placed her case on the contemporary bed and motioned to another door. "That's the bathroom. There's an indoor-outdoor pool just outside your window. The house was cleaned and stocked with food while we were"—he paused—"celebrating."

Kim allowed her eyelids to close, separating her from the reality of the day. Perhaps she'd wake up in her own apartment—the cool, yellow one, minus Nicholas A. Santos's large body.

When she opened her eyes, Nick was studying her darkly, his well-formed mouth grim. He sauntered toward her and took her heels from her hand, then studied her rumpled clothes. "You look like you need someone to take care of you, little girl," he murmured. "Damn," he cursed sharply, running the pad of his thumb beneath her eyes. "You look ready to collapse."

"I can manage," she sighed, not wanting him to see her vulnerability. She'd taken care of her own needs for years; she didn't want him looking down at her with that curiously compassionate look. It had probably already melted an army of women. The down coverlet on the bed beyond Nick's broad shoulders looked as fluffy and inviting as a cloud. She took a deep breath and started to move past him to her nightcase. Her feet ached from the high heels and she knew she limped. "Please leave. Go tuck your little metal monster in for the night or something."

"Your claws are showing, kitten. I think I like that. And by the way, I use my elbows."

Kim looked at him blankly. "So I won't crush my women," he teased. Nick hesitated for a millisecond, then scooped her into his arms, carried her to the bed, and gently sat her down. Kim swayed, feeling as if she would slide onto the floor like melted butter from a hot spoon. Nick's fingers wrapped about her left upper arm, steadying her.

The line of his mouth fought a smile as he looked down at her. "Okay, little girl. Relax. Papa's going to put you to bed," he said, and Kim yawned tiredly, aware of the deep humor in his tone.

"I can do it by myself . . ." she began sleepily as his fingers eased the mauve orchids from her hair and placed them on the night stand. There was something in the gentle firmness of his hands that reassured her. As if she were a child, Nick slipped her dress jacket from her. Kim protested his hands moving over her, replacing her clothing with something feather-light and silky. He drew back the coverlet on one side of the bed and eased her onto the heavenly sheets.

"Nick, you don't have to . . ." she murmured, as the thought that she'd never felt anything as wonderful as this flat surface filled her brain. As she sank onto the smooth sheets, Nick's weight depressed the bed as he sat, his fingers kneading her aching feet over her nylons.

Eyes closed, she heard his deep intake of air as she sighed and wriggled down into the mattress. The movement helped him slip off her pantyhose.

Nick stared at the limp garment, his throat drying instantly. "Damn. This is a first for me. I thought I could handle it better," he muttered, chafing his jaw. Exposed by the nightgown's neckline, the soft rise of her left breast seemed to roll as she curled to her side. Nick breathed lightly, his throat dry as he watched her long hair fall away from her slender neck.

When awake, Kim's blue eyes lashed at him or regarded him with all the warmth of an icicle. Now she looked like a woman who needed a man—him. God, how he wanted to lie down and fold her in his arms.

Sometime later, Kim stirred beneath the coverlet, drawing it over her head to muffle the awful sound. But the man's terrifying scream ricocheted again through the fabric, and a thump on the other side of the bedroom walls rattled the hanging pictures.

For a moment, Kim stared at the ceiling, noting the reflection of the pool's water dancing upon it. Then something shattered on the other side of the wall, and she threw back the coverlet, leaping to her feet. Bright sunlight entered the off-white shirred drapes, touching the lush jade carpeting of the bedroom. Dressed in her peach shortie gown, Kim remembered Nick's hands moving over her, sliding the gown over her bra and panties and lifting her long hair free. She remembered, too, the drowsy security surrounding her as he murmured directions to her. It was a warm, fuzzy feeling— as though someone cared. *Coming home . . .*

The sunburst gilt wall clock had read eight o'clock before another cry sent Kim running into the bedroom next to hers.

The huge round bed was a mass of tangled black satin sheets, pillows, and Nick's lean brown body. Mirrors lining the walls multiplied the man's limbs thrashing against the fabric. A large pottery lamp lay shattered on the white shag carpet, and a half-emptied bottle of whiskey and a glass stood on the bedside table. Nick's tuxedo and shirt were folded carefully over the back of a chair, his polished shoes placed neatly in front of it. Incredibly, the muted strains of *Bolero* floated over the disaster and an erotic movie played silently on the wall-sized screen over the bed.

"Not the kids!" Nick yelled, throwing out his arm and fighting the mass of satin sheets. Nick's nude body was nut brown from his neck to his heels as he flipped to his stomach. Unable to move, Kim stared at his tapering, rippling back. He half turned and Kim saw his hard buttocks and his upper thighs. Scars, old and white, lashed the sun-tanned flesh.

"Nick," she called softly, watching the nightmare terror spread across his hard face. When his mouth opened in a silent scream, Kim edged toward the bed and shook his shoulder. "Nick, you're dreaming. Wake up."

Nick's arms snaked around her, drawing her into the tangled web of sheets and man. He sweated, trembling, as he clung to her, his legs thrashing as if he ran, zigzagging through a mine field. "Hold tight, baby. I'll get you to a doctor. Hold on!"

His strength denied her efforts to free herself, and, wrapped in his nightmare, Nick cradled her head to his chest, his thighs working against the bed feverishly. "We'll get there, baby. We'll get there."

"Nick, Nick," Kim whispered urgently. Finally easing one hand to his head, she cradled his jaw and stroked it gently. "Nick, everything is all right. You're dreaming, Nick," she said soothingly, feeling his powerful legs slow their nightmare run.

"Hold tight, baby," he urged more slowly, his expression less fierce.

Kim closed her eyes, took a deep breath, and wrapped both her arms about his neck, tangling her legs with his, crooning to him, rocking her body against his larger one. "It's okay, Nick. You're fine now, Nick," she singsonged. "I'm here now. I'll take care of you. It's all right," she continued softly.

Nick groaned—a belly-wrenching groan—shuddering as Kim stroked the back of his neck, soothing the tight cords. She smoothed his curly hair, aware of it tangling silkily in her fingers. Tracing circles on his temples with her fingertips, Kim felt his muscled arms relax about her.

"It's okay, darling," she repeated, wondering momentarily why the endearment had slipped past her lips. The thong securing Nick's eye patch slipped and beneath it, his swarthy flesh was reddened and chafed. Kim's fingertips traced the line, soothing it.

Nick's body went still, his breathing leashed. His eye opened in an ebony blaze down at her. "What the hell are you doing, lady?" he asked tightly. His hands captured her wrists as his torso pinned her to the bed. His thighs clamped hers as Nick scowled down at her. He shook her gently, forcing her wrists beside her head. "Why are you in my bed, Goldilocks?" he asked more softly, as the nightmare shredded away and he was left holding Kim's stiff body.

She was frightened, he thought. Badly frightened. Her blue eyes were wide open and her face was pale. But damn, she was one hell of a soft woman, lying beneath him. He leaned closer, feeling the unbound softness of her breasts beneath the thin fabric of her gown, and the silky warmth of her thighs against his bulkier ones. He gathered both wrists into his right hand and lowered his left palm to stroke her hip. His desire was reaction to his dream, the need to bury himself in her and forget the war.

Her skin was satiny, the length of her thigh strong and smooth. He breathed shallowly, smelling the clean scent of her, watching her tongue slide over her soft bottom lip, moistening it.

"Nick," she whispered, trembling. "You've been dreaming. I just . . ."

"I know it," he barked, glaring at her. At that moment, still torn by the memories, Nick felt ragged, off-balance, and angry. She had intruded into his nightmare and he wanted her to pay for slipping into the inner recesses of his fears. No one had been there before.

Her soft mouth trembled. "Your scars . . ."

"Pretty, aren't they? Shrapnel makes all sorts of neat cuts," he snapped. Damn, why was she looking so wounded? As if she'd stepped into the very center of his nightmares?

"Was it so very bad?" she asked gently, sadness written in her glistening eyes.

"It was hell." She moved against him and Nick became aware of his weight covering her. He eased to one side, watching her expressions intently. He'd seen her scathing looks, her cool glide through self-possession as he'd teased her, but the expression in her beautiful face now knocked the wind out of him. Kim's closed lashes were damp, her face vulnerable.

"Nick," she whispered achingly, "I am so sorry."

Sorry? Nick barely breathed, knowing his thumb treaded the softness of her inner wrist. Sorry?

"It's over now, Kim," he said. "I'm awake." Why was she crying?

"Your scars . . ." She caught her bottom lip, tearing at the softness with her teeth. "Your eye . . . what you must have endured."

Fascinated by the single tear sliding from her right eye, watching it trail across her temple and into the silky curls, Nick was stunned. Kim was crying for him! He felt like an invisible fist had punched him in the gut. "It's over now," he repeated. He wanted to wrap her in cotton-wool and bind her to him.

When another tear followed the trail of the first one, Nick felt as helpless as a baby. He swallowed to push moisture down a suddenly dry throat.

"Hey, lighten up, will you?" He turned his mouth into a half smile, feeling as if he'd been knocked flat on his rear. "You're scaring the hell out of me."

When she managed a wobbly smile, Nick's stomach was filled with butterflies. "Lady, you can sure pull punches," he groaned, easing her against his side. He stroked her hair, felt her tremble against him, and knew he'd fight the war again to keep her.

"I'd better go back to my own bed," she breathed shakily.

"Uh-uh. You're staying put for now," Nick spoke against her sweetly scented hair. "You want to keep the bogeyman away, don't you?"

"You were frightening." The softness of her cheek moved on his chest as she spoke and Nick jumped slightly, feeling the pleasure wash over him. "Is it always this way?"

He caressed the sweep of her back. "Always. Sometimes worse." Why did his pain seem to melt away as he held her?

Kim yawned, and her breath fluttered through the hair on his chest. "Really, Nick. I've got to go back to my own room. I mean, how would it look . . ." Her low, husky voice slurred.

He smiled into her hair, covering her with the black

satin sheet. "It would look like we're married, lucky lady."

"Ummmm," she sighed sleepily. "I hope every day isn't like this one. And don't think this will happen again, mister. You'll have to fight your bogeyman by yourself."

He pressed his arm against her back, feeling her breasts flatten against his ribs. Damn. Kim Santos was his wife. Every delectable inch of her cuddly body. He grinned again. He didn't know who he liked better—yesterday's sultry, stream-heated lady, or the trusting one whose breath now feathered across his chest.

Kim stirred uneasily, her eyelids too heavy. She struggled to raise them. Sensing she was being watched, she scooted next to the large hard object in the water bed. It grunted, and, in the turning, tugged the sheet from her. Kim grabbed the edge of the sheet and pulled hard, dislodging another grunt.

"Oh, my God," she murmured, realizing she was in Nick's bed. Before she had recovered from that realization, she detected a motion from the corner of her eye and saw a handsome blond man staring at her, his hand wrapped about the doorknob.

"Oh, there he is," the man said easily, grinning. "We've been looking for him."

Kim drew the sheet across her chest, thrusting out her palm. "Now, listen. This isn't what it looks like—" she began. "He has bad dreams . . ."

Leaner than Nick but just as tall, the man's green eyes sparkled good-humoredly at her. "Uh-huh, honey. And you're his security blanket. Why don't you give him a pinch on the rear? He's apt to sleep all day and it's eleven o'clock now. Chow time for his daughter. She's running around the place like a wild Indian right now," the man stated in a Texan drawl. "Happy as a bee in a flower patch."

"Mornin', Duke. Meet the little woman." Nick yawned and spooned Kim into the cove of his body, his arm crossing her back to pin her to him. His big hand locked to the curve of her waist. "Sorry you had to be away when we got married. I could have used a better best man. Fletch dropped the ring."

"Uh-huh, but I had a merger in Dallas that couldn't wait, old buddy. You work fast for an old man." Duke winked.

"I'm not all that old, buddy," Nick stated flatly. Then he asked easily, "Can't you get your kicks without leering at my bride?"

Kim pulled the satin sheet over her head. "Nick . . ."

Nick shifted upright, his palm resting familiarly on the curve of her derrière. Her muffled, "Keep your hands to yourself, Nick Santos," brought a masculine round of chuckles.

Nick patted her bottom affectionately. "Okay, sweetheart. Anything you say."

"How about a drink with your buddy to celebrate, Nick?" Duke asked somewhere beyond the sheet. Liquid splashed into a glass and Kim winced—was this a male convention?

Nick's palm smoothed the satin sheet covering her hips in a blatant caress as he said, "Stay awhile, Duke. Cherry will find us soon enough."

A chair creaked and Duke sighed deeply. The water bed settled as if he had propped his boots upon it. Wonderful, Kim thought. A virtual male summit meeting. She heard the liquid splash again and hissed, "Get him out of here, Nick."

"In a minute, Mrs. Santos. We won't have time to talk when Cherry finds us. Ouch! Damn, you've pinched a piece out of me, sweetheart. Take it easy, will you?"

"I'll do more than pinch, Santos, if you don't get your Texan buddy out of here," she threatened darkly.

"Man, oh man. Who would have ever thought Nick Santos could get hog tied in less time than it takes to pluck a chicken?" Duke asked wonderingly. "This room looks like World War Three, buddy," he mused. "Must have been a hell of a wedding night."

"Yep." Nick's single word contained more male arrogance than an entire army. "She's a find, Duke." Nick patted her hip as if it was the bumper of his prized Porsche. "Chased me down and forced me to marry her . . . ouch! Damn, now that hurts, sweetheart. Stop it."

"You stop hurting my daddy, Kim," warned a child sharply, and Kim lifted the sheet to see Cherry's jam-smeared face glaring at her from the foot of the bed. She climbed onto the bed and crawled between Kim and Nick. Dressed in jeans, a T-shirt, and sneakers, Cherry sat astride Nick's broad chest. "You don't have to put up with this, Daddy. I'm smaller and I'd take less room than her," she announced. "She's got a room anyway. The bed's mussed up and I saw her clothes everywhere."

"Hey, buddy. What's the deal?" Duke asked curiously.

"None of your business, buddy," Nick stated darkly.

"Nick, do something. Now," Kim groaned, easing away from the loose circle of his arm. She was furious. Disheveled and displayed like a badly gift-wrapped package, she desperately wanted to flee, to escape to somewhere beyond the ranchette, where the world was filled with sane people.

"Nana!" Cherry yelled. "Nana, they're in here!" She eyed Kim distrustfully. "My grandma won't like it if you pinch my daddy."

Nick groaned. "Pour me another shot, Duke."

"Hold it right there, Nicholas. It's almost noon and I've already got coffee brewing. You're giving your bride a bad impression of the Santos family. Heavens! And Duke, you get yourself out of here," the woman's voice ordered the Texan as easily as if he were a large tabby cat.

Kim peered at the foot of the bed to see a small black-haired woman with snapping black eyes.

"My mother, Maria, sweetheart. Mom, meet Kim,

my wife." Nick relaxed back against the king-sized pillows.

"Nice to meet you, dear. Duke picked me up at the airport and, since the ranchette was on the way to the casino, we just dropped in. We'll give you a few moments with Cherry and we'll be on our way. Oh, dear, I'm so sorry . . . these two boys have absolutely no manners." She glared at Duke. "Get going, young man. We'll go all through the niceties later. Heavens!"

When Duke and Maria had gone, Cherry studied Kim solemnly. She toyed with the black curls covering her father's broad chest. She stared at Nick and laced her fingers with his. "I didn't know I was getting a real live-in mommy and a house, Daddy."

"I thought it would be nice for you to wake up this morning and find you have both, little broad. You've always wanted them. Like when you wake up on Christmas morning to new presents," Nick answered gently.

Kim felt sorry for the little girl. Apparently when Nick made decisions, he carried them out regardless of the consequences. Cherry unlaced her fingers from Nick's and touched Kim's wedding ring. "Pretty," she said, her eyes wary. "Are you really going to be my mommy?"

Kim ached, the emptiness rolling in her chest for her own lost little girl. She'd really wanted children, and if ever a child needed a mother's love, Cherry did. She turned her hand and clasped the smaller one. "We're going to have fun, Cherry. There are lots of things mommies and daughters do together."

Cherry chewed her lip, considering. "Like bake cookies?"

"Uh-huh." Kim smiled, her heart feeling full as the little girl's mouth moved in a small grin, her eyes sparkling.

"Like make doll clothes?"

"Uh-huh."

"Like going puppy-shopping?" Cherry ventured.

When Kim winked, Nick's daughter scrambled down from the bed, grinning. "This is going to be great, Daddy."

Nick yawned and stretched, eyeing Kim beneath his lashes. "I think so, little broad. I know I'm looking forward to it."

CHAPTER FIVE

"YOU'VE AVOIDED ME as though I had leprosy for two days, Kim," Nick snapped, glancing at his wristwatch. "It was Thursday morning when I brought you home. It's now Saturday, and you've managed to use the size of this house and your own room to avoid talking to me. Hell, even when we're in the same room, you're somewhere else. Everyone thinks we're having a little honeymoon—getting to know each other better. That's a laugh."

His gaze shot down, then up the length of her body as she leaned against the rec-room doorway. He was spoiling for a fight with her and he knew it, his body tense against the couch cushions. "Three o'clock in the morning is a long time since we shared that sprout salad of a lunch. And you've been hiding in your room until now. By the way, what type of man have you known who eats that grass instead of meat and potatoes?" Without waiting for her answer, he continued, "You can't stay holed up in that bedroom playing dance music for the duration." Nick stared at her as she stood in the shadows of the room. He jerked the video-recorder earplugs from his head, jabbed the remote-control button marked "Normal" and let Dracula's growls penetrate the well-equipped entertainment room.

Dressed in a hot pink body suit with a matching

headband and knitted leg warmers, Kim rubbed the
towel against her flushed cheek. Her ponytail clung
damply to her throat, encircling it. Nick watched her
dancer's glide to the couch beside him. Her eyes flicked
to the enormous screen. "Don't snarl, Nick," she stated
lightly. "I'm not used to cooking for anyone but myself,
nor am I used to an upside-down day. Normally, I'd be
sleeping soundly now. I've been working out. It helps
me think."

"I can think of a better way to work out," Nick muttered to himself, trying to conceal his frustration. He
wasn't used to being treated lightly and the feeling
chafed. Nor was he accustomed to women avoiding
him. Especially his wife. And damn it, Kim was his
wife. "Where's your wedding ring, Mrs. Santos?" he
asked her.

Kim sat at the other end of the sofa from him. She
crossed her legs lotus-style and wiped the back of her
neck with the towel. She watched the wide screen as
Dracula sank his fangs into his new bride's throat. "I
always liked this movie, especially the part where they
sink a wooden stake into his evil heart." She leveled a
meaningful stare at Nick. "Your ring is very valuable,
Nick," she continued. "It must have cost a fortune. I
don't intend for it to go down the garbage disposal. I'll
wear it when there's a need."

Nick pressed his lips together. He couldn't fight her
and the pain in his thigh. He rubbed the familiar pain
through his dress slacks, stretching his leg out on the
beige and blue couch.

Kim's eyes skimmed his face and traveled over his
opened white silk shirt. He noted she glanced uneasily
away from his exposed chest. He rather liked the wari-
ness in her expression—as if she hadn't known many
men physically, and he'd disturbed her cool facade.

"Have you been to the casino?" she asked in that
even tone Nick knew signaled her smoldering anger.

Nick kicked off his shoes. "Yes."

"I thought we'd settled that," she said tightly. "I

work there, too. You should have let me know you were going to work."

He glared at her. Dracula may have been the happiest at the midnight hour, but *he* definitely was not. "It would have been damned hard to explain my happy bride going to work so soon. That's why my mother is keeping Cherry at the casino suite. So we can have some privacy."

Her eyebrows raised. *"You* went."

Nick suddenly realized how few times women had challenged him in his life. He wasn't certain he liked the feeling. "That's different. I have an interest in seeing that the casino runs smoothly. And I'm not used to my bride hiding from me."

"My, my, Mr. Santos. Perhaps you're not the only one having difficulty adjusting to the situation." She glanced down at his hand gripping his thigh and frowned. "Are you in pain?"

Nick took a deep breath and thought: Oh, hell, she'd seen the effects of his nightmare after all . . . "Yes. But I'm staying off pain killers. I can live without them."

Her gaze trailed over his face slowly and coolly. "I see. Macho men bite the bullet. Is that right?"

"You're baiting me," he growled, wanting to drag her into his arms. Oh, hell, he thought again before he pulled her into his arms. He was tired and hurting and raw. His instincts told him this woman could salve his pain.

Nick's mouth was on hers, demanding, before Kim could react.

Pinned full length beneath his hard body, she had expected his mouth to ravish hers. She saw his thick eyebrows meet in a deep, almost painful frown, the soot-colored lashes forming a fan that brushed her cheek. The scent of lime after shave and Nick's earthy masculinity swirled about her senses. The stubble on his chin scraped her jaw as his mouth settled more lightly upon the contours of hers. Nick's groan was a surrender as his mouth lifted and fell, worshiping, savoring hers. "So soft, lady mine."

He inhaled a ragged breath and the movement brought the broad planes of his chest against her breasts. Turning her in his arms, Nick lay beside her, nuzzling her neck.

Thinking she must have lost her sanity, but suddenly unable to fight him, Kim closed her eyes and gave her mouth to his.

"Oh, God. Hold me, Kim," he demanded unevenly moments later. "Don't fight me."

His desperate tone jarred Kim from the sensual mists and she studied the hard-boned angles of his face on the pillow they shared. "Nick?"

Cradling his jaw with the palm of her hand, Kim ran a forefinger over the curls about his ear. He was big and tough, and now, she sensed, he was vulnerable.

He needed her.

The thought electrified Kim. Nick more than desired her body; he needed her. No one had needed her essence—the heart of her, her strength—in her entire life. The feeling was frightening, awesome, like free falling through the sky before opening a parachute. It was also a tender emotion that was not in her experience.

He turned to kiss her hand and his gaze tangled with hers. His big hand flattened low on her spine, warming her through her body suit. His right hand stroked her back gently, lightly. He grinned uncertainly, and Kim felt her heartbeat begin to accelerate.

"I didn't mean to grab you, lucky lady." His deep voice was husky and hesitant. He didn't move, his body tense, as if he were afraid to break the spell weaving around them. "Don't be frightened, Kim. You look wide-eyed and pale," he said more roughly. "I won't hurt you."

Kim stared at him, her mind racing over her thoughts. "I'm not frightened of you, Nick. I never have been."

He studied her face. "Brave little girl," he drawled at last, his smile deepening with confidence once more. "I could eat you for breakfast, Goldilocks."

She tapped his nose lightly with the tip of her index finger. "Bears can be gentled, my good man. Be careful."

She smiled at the thought of Nick tamed to her hand. Impossible.

His eye darkened as he concentrated on her cheek, his fingers smoothing it. "I've hurt you. You've got skin like flower petals and I've scraped it with my damned heavy beard."

Skimming her flesh, his fingertips left a path of tingling awareness, and she felt her stomach turn over. In this mood—gentle, caring, curious, needing—Nick was extremely dangerous to her.

She shifted in his arms and her thighs brushed his. He frowned quickly, easing back from her. "There's a piece of shrapnel still in there, sweetheart. Once in a while, it likes to act up."

Kim eased herself from his arms, steadying her shaking emotions. "Why don't you have it taken out?"

Nick's lashes lowered and he sighed deeply. "By the time the doctors discovered they'd missed the fragment, I'd had enough of surgery. I'm not going back."

She wanted to help him, ease him through his pain. "Could I help you?"

Without waiting for a reply, she eased his thighs across her lap, kneading gently, straightening his legs, warming his muscular legs lightly with her hands. Nick stilled, placing his arms behind his head as he watched her concentrate on his legs. "I could get used to this, little girl," he drawled.

"Does it really help, Nick?" she asked with concern.

"Damned right."

After a moment, she asked, "Better?" Nick's legs were heavy and she kept her ministrations low on his thighs, but he shifted slightly and her strokes almost touched him intimately.

"I could get used to the obedient-wife routine, Kim. I like your hands on me." His voice held an intimacy that spoke of silky nighties and bare flesh tangled on a round water bed.

She slid from beneath his thighs, standing and stretching. "Don't get too used to it. I'm not in the mood for that love swamp you call a bedroom."

When his eyebrows lifted questioningly, Kim's senses leaped. She'd just let Nick too close to her again and she knew he desired her. She didn't intend to have her emotions counted in the notches on his bedpost.

"I'd give a hell of a lot to know what's going on in your head right now, lucky lady," Nick stated as he stood upright slowly. "You've got that tight little expression that says you've made up your mind to do something. Someday I'll be able to read you better." He ran his fingers through the hair on his chest and Kim's eyes unwillingly followed the motion, her own fingers tingling. "How about going for a ride?" he asked unexpectedly.

Kim would have agreed to anything to relieve the tension she was feeling. "In your metal monster? You've ridiculed my Ford to the limits. You practically hid it in the garage."

Later, sitting behind the wheel of the powerful Porsche parked in the ranchette driveway, Kim turned to Nick. "No way am I driving this thing."

He frowned, the dawn's pink light burnishing the harsh angles of his face. "Is the seat belt too tight, Kim? Isn't the seat adjusted far enough forward for you? You understand the gears, don't you?" he asked anxiously.

"Nick," she began to explain for the second time since he'd placed her behind the wheel. "I like slow-paced, automatic cars. Ones with simple dials and little motors."

He stared at her blankly, then grinned in the shadows. "You'll get used to it. Just push the clutch in when you shift. It's easy; you'll love it when you get the hang of it. This baby practically drives itself. Push the clutch in." He placed his palm over the back of her hand, running her through the different gears. "An automatic shift can't compare. You can't feel the car work, be a part of it. Come on—start her up."

He scowled at her when the grinding sound stopped. "Turn the key *all* the way. You'll ruin the starter brushes."

Obviously, Nick was sharing his pride and joy with her. He was as animated and excited as a young boy sharing his prized toys, and Kim struggled through the gears until they reached an open highway.

Nick sighed, the desert air stroking his hair, the distant mountains looming like sentinels in the early morning dawn. From the side of the road, a coyote watched them travel the deserted highway.

He leaned forward scanning the horizon. "Shift down for that stop sign. Damn it! Shift down—it's easier on the brakes." When she complied, he eased back into the bucket seat with a deep, satisfied breath. "Great, huh? A beautiful morning. I can smell the sagebrush—Nevada's called the Sagebrush State, you know."

Yeah, a great morning, Kim thought, noting the perspiration dampening her T-shirt.

"Purrs like a kitten, doesn't she?" he asked, grinning at her. Kim concentrated on the too-narrow highway, aiming the mechanical beast down her side of the road.

"I don't know when I've had so much fun, Nick," she grumbled.

"I knew you'd like it." He chuckled. "We'll have to get you one."

"Not a chance. In the first place, I'm not taking gifts from you, and in the second place, I don't want any car with a mile of hood in front of it." Kim's fingers knotted about the customized steering wheel until they ached. Her thighs hurt with the tension she felt each time she shifted gears.

An oncoming car swept out of the morning gray, charging at her with bright head beams. She closed her eyes just when she thought they'd collide. The car honked, she swerved, and Nick swore. He stared at her as if she were an alien trespassing on earth.

"You damned near hit them, Kim," he accused, the angles of his face as stark and unyielding as the country-side.

She glared at him, pulling over to the shoulder. The car shuddered and died as she turned the ignition off and tossed the key into Nick's hand. "You drive."

He watched her stalk around the hood of the car, then stood up, towering over her. "Where did you learn to drive anyway? Some corn field?"

"Nick, if you don't shut up, I'm going to jog home." Why had she allowed him to con her into driving the beast? He'd been so damned excited, that's why, she answered herself. And she'd fallen for it, catering to him like every other woman he'd known.

"We're miles from the house, kitten," he purred confidently.

Without answering, Kim launched into an even running stride, her jogging shoes biting into the sand. She ignored his sharp call, "Kim, you get back here!"

The next afternoon, a Sunday, Maria watched Cherry carry out a plate of freshly baked granola cookies to Nick. He and Duke lay sprawled across loungers by the pool, enjoying the unusual warmth of the late April day. "She's awfully proud of making those cookies, Kim. It was sweet of you to take the time to help her. It's also sweet of you to let me stay with you for my vacation. I hadn't planned to have a new daughter-in-law when I arrived. But I'm so happy for you and Nick."

Kim smiled. "I'm glad you're here. We would have had to find someone to stay with Cherry while we're at work. So you see, it works out perfectly."

She watched as Nick looked up in surprise at his daughter, his grin a white flash against his dark skin. The warmth written in his expression made her heart turn over. Nick, the family man—Nick, the vulnerable man needing her—Nick, boyishly excited as he lectured her on the Porsche. He was devastating to her scarred and locked emotions. She swallowed, feeling shaky with the knowledge that he wanted her more than sexually. The minister's words echoed in her mind—"To have and to hold from this day forth." But their co-existence was temporary—she had to maintain her emotional balance or she stood the chance of being hurt again.

Maria's fingers wrapped about Kim's hand as it clung to the kitchen counter. Kim stared down at the wrinkles and the age spots, thinking how much her family differed from Nick's affectionate one. Physical closeness was not a part of her parental background. She noted the warmth in the members of the Santos family when they touched.

"I know the situation, dear. Nick explained the circumstances to me." Maria spoke softly as she patted Kim's hand. "I realize this isn't a real marriage, but Cherry is excited about having a real home and her own mother, and Nick's positively glowing. Laura can't help but see how well suited you are for each other. You know, I never really did like that girl."

She winked at Kim as she lifted the granola cookies from the baking sheet to a cooling rack. "In fact, you may be just what Nick needs. He's been getting a little stiff lately. You know, a little too hard shelled to suit me. You've got just enough spit in you to make him sit up and take notice."

"Maria, catching Nick for a permanent husband is the last thing I want," Kim stated, then amended, "Not that he wouldn't make someone happy. He's just not my type."

"Opposites attract, dear." Maria patted Kim's hand again.

"What opposites, Mom?" asked Duke, rambling into the kitchen dressed in his cutoffs and Stetson. As tall as Nick, the younger man's eyes bore a constant mischievous twinkle.

"Oh, Duke. We're talking girl talk. You wouldn't be interested," Maria said, neatly sidestepping his question. She shrugged. "You wouldn't understand about mixing health foods and spaghetti anyway."

"Uh-huh," he agreed flatly, allowing himself to be sidetracked as he reached for a cookie. "But I do know that Nick let Kim drive his Porsche."

"No, you don't mean it!" Maria declared, staring at Kim disbelievingly. *"No* one drives Nick's cars."

Kim felt a flush rise to her cheeks and wished she had more covering her than her lime green polka-dot bikini. "He forced me. I haven't driven a stick shift since our farm trucks. I ground the gears, and he yelled. He yelled at me," she said again, remembering. In her experience, emotions were tightly controlled. But Nick's temperament was like sparks to tinder—he made her flame, unable to predict her own reactions.

Duke munched on his cookie. "Nick loves his cars, Kim. He believes they're like women. Give 'em what they need and they'll roll—"

"Duke, mind what you're saying," Maria interrupted sharply. "You can't have any more cookies if you don't behave."

The Texan's green eyes widened. "Now, Mom. I've been a good buddy of Nick's since Nam. You wouldn't deny me a few cookies, would you?"

Maria scowled up at him and tapped him in the stomach with a wooden spoon. "I mean it, Duke. Behave."

Cherry's giggle brought Kim's eyes to Nick who stood in the doorway holding his daughter's hand. His black swimsuit covered little of his lean hips and her mouth went dry, her fingers clinging to the edge of the counter for support. His gaze melded with hers, the hot desire written in his face. Water dripped from his hair onto his chest, the drops glistening in the dark wedge of hair flowing downward to his flat stomach. His scars had turned purple in the slight chill of spring, barely recognizable in his bulky thighs.

He surveyed her body with obvious intent, his expression hardening as he glanced at Duke, lounging against the counter near Kim.

"Daddy wants more of my cookies, Nana," Cherry chirped, dancing toward her grandmother.

Duke picked the little girl up and sat her on the counter, his eyes meeting his friend's blazing stare with open curiosity. "Hey, buddy. What gives?" he asked, his eyebrows lifting.

"Not a damn thing . . . buddy," Nick answered him, stalking toward Kim. Too gently his large hand collared her bare neck beneath her hair. "Hello, bride." His thumb cruised the angle of her jaw and neck in a slow sweep as he raised her mouth for his hot, sensuous kiss.

When his lips lifted, he held her confused stare. Kim felt the shock of his kiss down to her bare toes as they curled on the kitchen carpeting. He tasted—primitive. As if he were branding her.

"Daddy?" Cherry's high-pitched tone entered Kim's confusion.

"Uh-huh, little broad?" Nick smiled at his daughter easily and wrapped an arm around Kim's bare waist to draw her to him. Nestled in the crook of his arm, her hips touching his blatant maleness, Kim shivered. His fingertips stroked the indenture of her waist.

Cherry's small face bore a hurt expression and Kim instinctively reached out for her, cradling her on her hip. The child's eyes were huge, her thumb sucked into the vacuum of her mouth. Kim kissed her cheek and nuzzled her hair, sensing Cherry's need for reassurance. "We're going to have so much fun, Cherry—all of us. Can I suck your thumb, too?"

Comforted, Cherry grinned widely. "I sucked all the good stuff out. There's no more left and I'm not sucking it anymore, Kim."

The little girl curled her arm about her father's neck and stroked his tense face. "Are all of us going to have fun, Daddy? Do you like to bake cookies, too? You look so . . . mean, Daddy. Is Uncle Duke a bad boy?"

Maria started to hum and sponge wipe the stove while Duke continued to stare at Nick as if he'd never seen his friend in this mood.

"Nick!" Kim protested, trying to move away from him. "You're cold."

Duke took Cherry from Kim. "Lighten up, buddy. You'll grind your teeth down to the gums if you don't stop."

Kim had the feeling she was trapped between two warring cavemen. "Duke," she asked lightly, "what kind of a car do you drive?"

"A Rolls with longhorns as a hood ornament. It's parked in the driveway."

"It's a big stick," Nick stated sharply. From the glare in his eye, Kim knew he referred primarily to the car's shifting mechanism and secondly to Duke's physique.

Half an hour later Kim changed into a sweater and jeans. Refusing to be drawn into Nick's and Cherry's championship Pac-Man battle, she walked Duke to his Rolls and inspected the huge horns protruding from either side of the silver hood.

"This car looks ridiculously long, Duke." She laughed, enjoying Duke's lighthearted temperament. "I'd never be able to park it."

Duke stroked the longhorns reverently. "It's a peach. Hey, kid"—his handsome face became serious—"I'm here if you need me, okay? Nick can play rough ball sometimes. You just have to understand where he's coming from. He's been through a lot."

"I can handle him. He is my husband, Duke." Husband—the word rolled strangely across her tongue.

"Hmmph. I was here on your wedding morning, kid. And when you changed clothes just now, you didn't use the master bedroom. Nick's acting like a starved groom and you're skittering around him. Something's not on the up and up. And unless I miss my guess, your marriage has something to do with Laura's bid for child custody. You know, the happy home scene—the little woman—"

"Don't pry, Duke," Kim warned.

"I agree," Nick interrupted behind her, slipping his arms around her waist to draw her back to him.

After Duke had gone, Nick turned her, his large hands cupping her shoulders. His expression was dangerous. "As far as you're concerned, little girl, I'm the only game in town. Understand?"

Kim shook free of his grasp, planting her fists on her hips. "Don't get any big ideas, Santos. Duke is a nice man and I enjoy his company."

His eyebrows drew together, his shoulders tensing beneath the white cotton T-shirt. His long jeans-clad legs took an arrogant stance. "Friends?" he scoffed. "Duke has laid every broad he's come close to."

She could feel the anger beginning to boil in her veins. Until she'd met Nick she'd been a cool determined career woman. She liked her life that way—it was safer. She thumped his broad chest. "I'm not a broad, Nick. Remember that."

"Hell! You're every inch a lady. But I'll bet that when the bedroom door closes you're sheer dynamite. The combination of lady and lover is every man's dream, Kim. Including Duke's."

"Well, you're safe," Kim rapped out. "I wouldn't have you if you were Diamond Jim!"

"Lady mine, you've already got me!"

Every atom in Kim's body felt charged up for a battle royal. No one had her. "Think again," she stated slowly and softly. She tapped her index finger against his broad chest, punctuating her words. "I've never liked the male possession routine, Nick. You can drop it when we're in private."

He scowled down at her. "I told you I didn't like bossy women."

"That's your problem, Mr. Santos."

He grinned slowly, knowingly. "Women—with the exception of my ex-wife—have never given me problems."

"Times have changed, Nick. If we're going to make

this charade work, you're going to have to quit acting like a jealous husband."

His grin died, replaced by a thoughtful expression. One black brow lifted. "Am I too much for you to handle?"

Kim glared at him for a moment, thinking of apt replies. Then she decided to retreat from the battlefield with what little sanity she could still salvage.

CHAPTER SIX

SHE'S GOING TO be mine all the way. It had been a week since he'd met Kim, Nick thought as he watched his wife survey the casino crowd. She was a beautiful, enticing, and exciting woman, and she glared at him each time he neared her. She acted as if he would purposely let his male hormones run amok at the sight and scent of her.

In the loving ruse of newlyweds at the casino, he readily used his advantage, kissing and holding her whenever he did manage to get close. Nick grinned. Hell, he'd never turned down an opportunity in his life, he thought as he started toward her.

Behind Kim, Nick slid his hands to her waist. He caught the gasp of surprise with his lips, turning her against him and wrapping her in his arms.

She tasted like a bonbon at Christmas time. Her lips parted and Nick slipped his tongue inside, trailing over the top row of her teeth, then delving into the warm moistness of her mouth.

For an instant, her palms thrust against his chest, but as Nick's hand slipped low on her spine, something went warm and lax within Kim. As her body flowed into his, Nick's body heated.

Realizing his control was about to slip away, Nick reluctantly ended the kiss, and his lips trailed over the warm contours of Kim's cheek to her ear. "Enjoying yourself, sweetheart?"

She tensed, easing back from him. The reflection of the casino's bright lights glittered in Kim's flashing blue eyes.

"You could at least let me see you coming," she scolded Nick, her left index finger shaking just below his nose. "In the week since I've agreed to this farce, Nick Santos, you've made me angry more times than I have ever been in my entire life. In fact, I never had a temper until I met you!" She waved her hand across the crowded casino. "You could have picked on anybody—this place is loaded with beautiful women. Why me?"

Nick leaned against the paneled wall. In the privacy of the secluded shadows and concealed by an enormous potted palm, he decided to let Kim rave at him. Dressed in a street-length red lamé gown with a sequined white flower covering one shoulder, Kim was in a fine rage. A flush underscored her golden-girl complexion; her long curls bobbed with each toss of her head. She looked, Nick thought, as if she wanted to take him apart.

Kim may have been able to keep everyone else on the perimeter of her inner emotions, but she sure as hell didn't keep cool around him. Her reactions were genuine and hot-blooded, stripped of cool pleasantries. Damn, he felt good. He smiled slightly, resting the impulse to break into a grin.

Her eyes widened. The long silky length of her legs locked into a defiant stance, tightening the glittering fabric about her hips and thighs. The rhythm of her shaking finger increased. "Don't you stand there and grin, you big ape. You installed a workout room in the house. Fine. Cherry and I can use it together. She's got all the makings of a good gymnast. And you definitely need to exercise your legs. I even understood why you got a stack of credit cards in my name—for appearance sake. But to go out and buy all these clothes—these expensive gowns," she corrected.

Her hand swept down the evening dress and Nick

appreciatively noted the rapid rise and fall of her full breasts. His admiring gaze stroked her waist and trim hips and along the slender curve of her thigh exposed by the slit. Kim was all woman. A passionate woman who was reading him the riot act like any other good wife might. And damn, if she didn't have the sweetest-tasting mouth, he'd decided just as Kim finished, ". . . to buy them without my permission is really too much."

He'd watched her work the casino the past five nights, admiring the easy way she handled irate or drunken women. One hefty woman who looked as if she'd been in every bar across the United States had grabbed Kim's long blond hair. Frightened for her, Nick had just started toward them when Kim had smiled that cool smile of hers and sent her elbow into the woman's bulbous stomach. Gently, she'd eased the winded woman into a secluded corner, talking and patting the customer's beefy shoulders. After a moment, the woman had attempted a wobbly smile and Kim had handed her some betting chips.

Against his better judgement, Nick just had to reach out and stroke the moist softness of her bottom lip with the pad of his thumb. Just once. Beneath his touch, Kim's lovely body trembled down its silken length. There was something hot and dancing in her each time he came near. It was no less powerful than the attraction he felt for her.

"When I'm gone, you won't be able to give these gowns to another woman," Kim began reasonably, and he watched her struggle for control. Her trembling fingers eased back the curls from her face, firmly rein-stating a tortoiseshell comb. "You did not have my per-mission to rummage through my clothes and lend my only evening dress to the dressmakers. These gowns are custom fitted and I'm too . . . too . . ." She swept her hand down the length of her body.

"Full breasted? With a tight end?" he offered teas-ingly. "I've noticed."

"Nick, you're entirely too fresh," Kim stated shakily.

"Fresh? Me? I'd like to be with you, honey. Your blush is doing some pretty exciting things to my chemistry."

"Huh! Your *chemistry* is too...too experienced. Nick!"

Aching for the feel of her satiny skin beneath his hands, he reached out, grasping her wrist before she could escape. He drew her against him, watching her soft mouth tremble and her eyes widen as he encircled her with his arms.

"Nick!" she protested, squirming within his embrace.

"A man can kiss his wife if he feels like it, can't he? In fact, it's expected once in a while, lady mine. I love it when you move against me, honey. Don't look so shocked—it'll only hurt for a little while."

When she'd relaxed, her mouth parted. Nick groaned. "I know you like to kiss me, honey."

Kim's tongue trailed across her bottom lip. "Part of the job is to—"

"Liar," he accused tenderly. Using the wall for support, Nick drew her into the cradle of his thighs. He loved the softness of her thighs moving between his splayed legs. He loved the purr of anticipation deep in her throat before his mouth closed over hers. When the tip of his tongue slid over the contours of her full mouth, she gasped and the movement raised her breasts against his chest. When her tongue timidly returned the play, Nick's knees went weak, his groin getting red-hot "activate" messages from his male senses.

She eased closer and Nick felt the earth move around them. His left hand slipped between them just as her arms rose to lock behind his neck.

Flattening herself to Nick's blatant need, Kim ached. She wanted to be a part of him, to hear his husky, hungry groans, to feel his uneven breath sweep warmly across her cheek. His hips rubbed sensuously against hers and Kim's reserve melted. Arching against him, she felt his large hand travel upward, seeking her breast.

Nick groaned, his kiss devouring, as he cupped her

softness with his palm. Kim pressed a trail of kisses
along his jaw, loving the taste of his roughened skin,
loving the heat rising in his cheeks. When she stroked
his tensed neck, Nick trembled, his right hand lowering
to smooth her hips through the fabric of her dress.

When his finger and thumb plied her nipple through
the cloth, heat waves swept over Kim. Rippling pleasure shot through her again and again.

"God! Let me have you, honey. I ached for you the
moment I saw you," Nick demanded roughly against her
cheek as he blazed a trail of kisses toward her earlobe.

He bent to nibble at her neck, arching her backward
over his arm. Reeling with his need, dazed by the caress
of his hand across her breasts, Kim felt reality spinning
out of reach. "Honey, don't fight me now," he urged
harshly. "I'll be very careful with you."

Kim barely heard his promise as she unfastened two
of his shirt buttons and slipped her hand inside. Fingers
curling into the crisp hair covering his chest, she found
his nipple and circled it with her fingertips. Nick almost
jumped. His gaze was a hot black blaze down at her.
"Lady. Did you know that men are almost as sensitive
there as women?" he asked sharply. "We could end up
on the casino floor."

"No, I didn't know that," Kim murmured, enchanted
by the stark look of helplessness and desire written on
his rugged features.

His fingers circled her wrist, drawing her hand from
him. He kissed her palm and pressed it to his jaw.
"Honey." He laughed shakily. "For a divorcée, you have
a lot to learn. Men have erogenous zones, too. And I'm
going to enjoy teaching you the finer points of lovemaking."

"You act as if my husband didn't teach me anything."

Nick's dark brows met in a frown. "I'll bet he didn't
know what to do with all that heat, Mrs. Santos. You
could scorch a man down to his . . ." He grinned rakishly, letting her mentally complete his sentence.

"Just what are you up to, Nick Santos?" she asked shakily.

"We could go home if you're feeling friendly. I *am* the boss, you know," he purred.

Kim liked the deep sound of his voice. The husky undertones raked at her feminine senses. His body was hard, waiting against hers, and Nick's intent gaze sharpened, probing her slight frown. "You're not ready yet, are you, lady? You're so damned used to holding in that you can't let go."

Kim weighed his words. Nick made her hot and wobbly and aching. But physical relationships were fleeting and loves were as dangerous as thin ice on a pond. "Just because we've shared a few kisses doesn't mean I'm ready to make any commitments, Nick. I don't sleep around."

"No one said you did. But I know if you gave yourself to me, you'd be making a serious commitment, and it scares the hell out of you, doesn't it?" he asked roughly, his hands spanning her waist.

She felt all the seeking desire, the hungry heat begin to shatter in him. Nick looked desperate, like a man on a thin leash. His stare locked with hers.

"Nick, you're pushing."

"Damn right. You're mine, lady. Lock, stock, and barrel. I want to take you to the suite upstairs and make love to you until you *can't* slide back into that cool little shell." His tone softened, and a teasing light entered his ebony eye. She sensed that he wanted to ease the harsh mood between them. He traced her nose with a fingertip. "If you let me have you, I'd let you drive my Porsche."

"Big deal. I hate the thing." She felt shaky, her stomach lurching. Nick was definitely flirting with her, trying to get her to respond in kind.

He kissed her nose, then placed his forehead against hers, rocking her against him easily. "You love it. You know you do, little girl," he purred. "In fact, you love a lot of things." His hips ground suggestively into hers.

"Mean old thing," she accused, glad for the lighter moment. "You're not a very good driving instructor. That was a long five-mile run with you following me in the car, looking like you wanted to throttle me."

"You pouted, little girl. Slammed doors and turned up your stereo so loud it rocked the house. You'll see, I'm better at teaching other things."

She peered at him through her lashes, liking his playfulness. If she were only in the market for a lover, Nick certainly had possibilities.

"How tacky, Nicky," purred a female voice behind Kim. "Love behind the potted palms? You used to find more appropriate places to ah . . . indulge yourself."

"Laura." Nick's grin died, replaced by a cold mask-like expression. He turned Kim, locking her within the circle of his arm.

His ex-wife's beautiful face hardened as she examined Kim. "I heard you'd gotten married suddenly, Nicky. Your wife?" She glanced down at his unbuttoned shirt. "Hungry for you, is she? Well, I was, too—once. God, she even looks like me. A blue-eyed blonde. Did you find a proper substitute, sweety?"

"Kim, meet Laura." Nick's voice bore a sharp edge, his fingers redoing his buttons. His right hand drew Kim closely to him.

When Kim extended her hand for a handshake, Laura looked at it as if it held manure. She straightened her lavender voile dress, and the heavy ruffle settled over her breasts, concealing the dark outline of her nipples. "Nicky, I've come for Cherry. Charles—my new husband—said to offer you any amount. He's expecting the dear little thing to come back with me to our suite at the Hilton. I have his checkbook right here, so could we get the transaction over with before he gets tired of waiting? The lawyers can clean up the paperwork later."

"Cherry is not for sale, Laura," Kim stated quietly before Nick could speak.

Laura lifted her left hand and studied the three-carat diamond weighting her finger. She stared at Nick, her mouth hardening beneath its glossy covering. "Oh, come now, Nick. Don't let this little *wife* of yours make you unreasonable. I'm willing to pay anything to please Charles. Surely you can't want that little brat underfoot all the time. She'd have a nanny and toys. What more could she want?"

Beside Kim, Nick's big body went tense. "Cherry has what she needs. More than that, she has love," he said.

"Oh, do spare me, Nicky," Laura hissed. "The kid is half mine. I need her for Charles. He adores kids. And he doesn't have the scars to make her have nightmares, either," she shot at him. She stared at Kim. "Beastly scars, aren't they, dear?"

Kim could feel anger vibrating from Nick. The line of his jaw jutted forward and his mouth clamped shut. No wonder he'd been curious about her reaction to his disfigurements. This viper had probably goaded him incessantly. Kim felt very protective of him suddenly. He needed her.

Her senses geared up. For an instant, she felt like the Fifth British Brigade charging to rescue the Alamo, and she didn't have time to analyze her impulses. She leaned against him slightly and laced her fingers with his tensed ones on her waist.

Nick relaxed slightly, glancing down at her. "It's okay, sweetheart. I don't beat women." To his ex-wife, he stated quietly, "I'm not arguing the point, Laura. She has a mother and a home. You gave up all rights to her when she was a baby."

"Oh, don't hand me that baby-has-a-mommy routine. It's positively sickening," Laura spat out, her blue eyes seeming to rip at Kim's controlled expression. "You just married this bimbo last week. I checked. She couldn't possibly have developed a rapport with Cherry in that amount of time. The kid will never miss her."

Nick took a threatening step forward, halted by Kim's hand flattened to his chest. She half turned toward him. "Darling, if Laura would like to inspect

Cherry's home, it's fine with me. Surely we can settle this calmly. But I can understand her apprehension," she said smoothly.

"Apprehension?" Laura's plucked brows rose. "You're the one who had better have apprehension. You just married a man who's still in love with *me*. He always has been. He picked you, honey, because you look like me. A fool could see the resemblance. He actually had the gall to act wounded when I couldn't stand those scars. So I took pity on him one night, and guess what happened? A kid. God, how I hated being fat."

Kim eased closer to Nick, snuggling intimately against him, her eyes locked with the other woman's. "Nick is my husband," she stated quietly. "I love him and I'll take any part of him I can get."

Laura's face turned pale and she glared down at their joined hands. "Aren't you cute? Yes, I want to see Cherry's happy little home. I'll make an appointment . . . before I start child-custody proceedings."

After Laura had gone, Kim eased her hand from Nick's big one. "I can understand why you think of her as a witch." She rubbed her fingers. "You almost broke my hand, Nick Santos. She really knows how to get to you."

A muscle contracted beneath Nick's normally swarthy cheek, and he swallowed. "Do you need a drink, Nick?" Kim asked.

"Hell, yes," he snapped. "That broad just starts talking about Cherry and I get mad."

In his office, Nick splashed a whiskey neat into a glass and drank it quickly. He stalked the confines of the thickly carpeted room like a nervous panther in a small cage. He took another tall drink and glared at Kim from beneath his brows.

Kim smiled confidently, concealing her concern. Nick looked thunderous, as if he wanted to break something. Anything. "Are you going to explode, mean old thing? You look like you might rate a nine on the

Richter scale if you did," she teased lightly, waiting for the eruption of the century.

He continued to glare at her, stalking toward her. Kim refused to be intimidated by his fierce expression. When he was inches from her, he cradled her jaw within his hands. "Mean and old, am I, lady? I could disprove that theory right on that couch over there. I'll show you I'm everything you ever wanted in a man."

Breathing unevenly, his frustration evident, he trembled. Kim placed her hands on his wrists and stroked them with her thumbs. "She's not going to get Cherry, Nick," she whispered.

He swallowed, his fingers shaking as they splayed across her cheeks and jaw. He hesitated, then asked urgently, "How do you know, Kim? She's a bitch, but she is Cherry's biological mother. Judges weigh that fact in custody cases."

"I thought you were brave, macho man. Green Beret and all that male ego stuff," she teased again. Then she added softly, "I'm here now, Nick. And I'll do my best not to let anyone hurt her." Kim continued to stroke his thick wrists, her fingertips resting over his quickly beating pulse.

Nick studied her upturned face carefully, his intense expression easing. "I don't scare you at all, do I?" A corner of his mouth lifted in a gentle smile. "By the way, honey. I'm not used to being defended the way you did with Laura. A man could thrive on your attention."

Kim frowned. There he went again. As soon as she let him past her defenses, he started prowling, hunting, stalking... "Don't get any big ideas, Santos. You wanted to convince Laura, and I was doing my job."

When she moved back from him, he frowned, continuing to scan her face. His big hands warmed her cheeks, his fingertips smoothing her temples. "Lonely lady. Who hurt you? Your husband?"

Nick's expression of concern unsettled her, convulsing her stomach. "Richard didn't care enough to really hurt me, Nick," Kim rapped out sharply. "Anyway, it's none of your business."

His concern turned to anger, his large fingers tensed upon her face. "It damned well is from now on, lady. I've fallen in love with you."

Fallen in love with you. Kim repeated the words inside her head for a moment, her bones beginning to liquify. No one fell in love anymore except in the movies, she thought.

He shook her head gently, his eye seeking hers. "Don't look so shocked, honey. It happens every day."

With a dry throat, Kim managed to say, "Not to me it doesn't."

His eyebrows lifted and Nick smiled his most engaging, most frightening smile down at her. "Try it. You'll like it."

"Not you," she gasped, sliding from his touch, turning from him. "Oh, no. Not you."

His arms encircled her immediately, sliding to pin her back against him. His tall body sheltered her trembling one as he rocked her side to side. "Don't be afraid, honey," he murmured in her hair. "You were a tigress defending her own against Laura. Think about that."

"No. I was simply doing a job, Nick."

"No way, honey. It's more than that. There's an expression in your face when you play with Cherry—soft, motherly, proud. You're attached to my daughter, and I come with the package. I'm going to get you, one way or the other. When you told Laura you loved me, I promised myself then that one day you'd really mean it."

"Don't wait around, Nick. You're entirely too possessive and manipulative. You gamble in games that concern other people's lives."

"And you like my kisses, lucky lady. You burn when I touch you."

"We have nothing in common, Nick."

His laughter was full-throated and Kim rounded on

him, her eyes flashing. "Don't you dare laugh, Nicholas A. Santos."

He reached to stroke her hot cheek. "Just wait, my passionate bride. You'll see exactly what we do have in common. By the way, the 'A' stands for accessible, lady."

His soft chuckle traveled down Kim's spine and raised goose bumps on her flesh before he left the room. Kim stood alone hugging herself and shivering. She'd successfully defended her emotions for years but now she had a premonition that Nick just might have the ability to hurt her again.

At eight o'clock the next morning, Kim tied the laces of her jogging shoes. She began her warm-up stretching exercises, preparing for her run. Exhausted emotionally, she'd finally settled down in the early hours to watch Humphrey Bogart and Katharine Hepburn pull the *African Queen* through the swampways and discard their leeches, and had finally slept a few hours.

Cherry, dressed in a T-shirt and shorts, leaned sleepily against Kim's doorway. "I wanna go run, too. Daddy and me got new shoes, so we can run with you. He says you're too pretty to run around by yourself. Somebody might steal you."

"Oh, he did, did he?" Kim asked more easily than she felt. Nick Santos certainly was rattling his possessive bones. "Don't worry about me, Cherry. I've been taking care of myself for a long time now."

The little girl eased closer to Kim, her wide blue eyes questioning. "Kim?"

"Uh-huh?"

"Tammy's dog had puppies. Her house is just down the road. She says her mom told her to give them away to anyone who wants one. I sure want one."

Kim felt the warmth surround her, the old emptiness of her own lost child easing each time she was near Cherry. She knelt beside the girl and hugged her. Cherry's arms flew around Kim's neck, and Kim felt her heart melting. "What do you think the odds are on getting your daddy to say yes, Cherry?" she asked, enjoying the little girl's soft cuddly warmth.

Cherry played with Kim's ponytail, smelling it. "Two to one. We can play the angles. You know, make Daddy happy. He likes our cookies."

Kim giggled. "Your daddy isn't easy to convince, Cherry. By the way, where is he?"

"Still sleeping. Nana says that Daddy didn't sleep good last night. We could go to Tammy's house this morning and get the puppy and surprise Daddy when he wakes up. Like he surprised me with a new mommy."

Indulging her own needs, Kim kissed Cherry's cheek. The little girl sighed and stared deeply into Kim's eyes. "I love you, Kimmy. Daddy says you're ours to keep now."

More easily than she felt, Kim smiled. In spite of her precociousness, Cherry needed comforting the same as any other little girl. Kim hugged her once more and patted her bottom. "Go get dressed. We'll go check out Tammy's puppies."

"My puppy, Kimmy."

Two hours later, wearing jeans and a yawn, Nick stalked into the family room. His rugged unshaven face was worn. He scowled down at Kim and Maria. Seated on the carpet, they watched Cherry crawl after her scampering puppy.

Maria glanced up at her son as he folded his arms ominously across his chest and leaned against a doorway. "There's a hell of a lot of noise out here for only ten o'clock in the morning."

"Oh, Nick. Were you able to sleep at all?" his mother asked anxiously. In a hushed tone, she said, "The nightmares will go away someday, son. You'll see."

"Yeah, sure. In the meantime, nobody has this much fun in the morning," he grumbled.

Maria rose and hugged him as she walked by. "You'll feel better after you eat, Nick. I'll go fix breakfast."

After she'd gone, Nick glared at Kim. "The dog just wet on the carpet, dammit."

Her eyebrows lifted. Nick may have had a bad night, but she certainly didn't intend to pay for it. Cherry was delighted with the puppy, and she wasn't going to let him ruin any part of his daughter's happiness this morning either. "Playing the part of Christmas Scrooge, Nick? Bah, humbug?" she asked lightly.

"Don't get wise, Kim. I'm not in the mood for it. What are you going to do about the puppy wetting all over everything?" he asked.

"Well, Nick. *We're* going to housebreak him. In the meantime, baking soda and water will help the stains on the carpet." She lifted a damp rag for his inspection, then wiped the wet spot.

"Now he's chewing on my morning paper, Kim," Nick stated darkly. "I assume it's a he, isn't it?"

Cherry's excited scream sounded just before the black and white puppy's oversized feet tangled in a lamp cord. The lamp slid from the table in a crash of expensive pottery.

"Hell!" Nick cursed, his jaw jammed down almost to his chest. "You marry a woman, let her drive your car when she doesn't know reverse from high gear, and she thinks she runs the place. I suppose this mess is your idea, Kim Santos?" he accused.

Kim could have outglared him. But Cherry was so happy, she didn't want to spoil a second of it. Kim opted for another route around Nick's obvious dislike of the puppy. She'd reason with him. She'd cajole him. It was a tactic that had worked well in his rage against Laura. And he'd accept the puppy in spite of himself. She stretched her legs in front of her and leaned back against the couch. "Cherry, would you please take your puppy outside to play? I'll take care of the lamp, and your daddy and I need to talk."

Cherry snatched the fat puppy into her arms, ready to defend it. "Lassie is mine now, Daddy," she said with a touch of the Santos arrogance.

"Lassie?" Nick's eyebrows rose, his head pivoting toward Kim's relaxed sprawl on the floor. "It's a female?"

"It's a male, dear. But for now, Cherry likes calling him Lassie," Maria said as she entered the room. She served coffee quickly, sparing a wink at Kim, then breezed out of the room. "Breakfast will be ready in a minute, you two," she called over her shoulder.

Nick's big hands wrapped about the steaming pottery mug. Kim balanced her coffee on her flat stomach and waited. The puppy yelped outside and Cherry screamed happily, calling after it.

"Listen to that racket," Nick complained, throwing himself onto the couch and easing his legs out in front of him. "Sounds like a damned circus. She can't keep it, Kim."

"Mmmm." Kim sipped her coffee and leaned back, rather enjoying Nick's discomfort as he fingered the damp shredded roll of his newspaper. "We'll get him a leather chew toy, Nick. He'll housebreak easily. Drink your coffee. And I'll take you for a drive."

"Whose car?" His wary tone caused Kim to smile.

"Mine. I'll drive," she said quietly, knowing Nick's reaction in advance.

"Like hell! Parts of it litter the highway. The color reminds me of old moss."

"I'll let you teach me how to drive the Porsche, Nick," Kim offered, peering at him from beneath her lashes. "I'll do better this time."

"Now that's a maddening offer. A chance to get you alone and let you tear up my car," he grumbled. His hand slipped down to stroke her neck idly. "You're sweaty."

"I've been jogging in place, watching Cherry bring the puppy home."

"I was going to run with you this morning, but my leg—"

"You don't have to jog with me, Nick." Kim didn't like the idea of Nick entering her contemplative runs.

Her privacy was limited enough. "Can Cherry keep the puppy?" she asked quickly to change the subject.

He sipped his coffee, toying with her ponytail. Suddenly, in one motion, he set his cup on the floor. Taking her mug and placing it beside his, Nick gathered her in his arms and rolled them across the carpet. "I'll wrestle you for it, honey."

Breathing heavily, pinned beneath Nick's heavy body, Kim felt her heartbeat shift into overdrive. Nick was rumpled and warm and too attractive, grinning down at her confidently. "You'd win. You're big as a house."

He nuzzled her neck, biting it lightly. "Mmm, I don't know. When you start flirting with me, I lose all sense of direction . . ."

"I do not flirt with you, Nick Santos. And stop breathing into my ear!"

His hips thrust down against hers. "I like it when you squirm. Then I stop thinking."

"You're being juvenile, Nick. And you're crushing me."

Rolling to his back, Nick cradled her on top of him. "Cherry can have the puppy if you'll give me one hell of a kiss, lucky lady. Put everything you have into it."

"You're an awful man, Nick."

"Awful," he agreed as his hand stroked down the length of her bare thigh, his fingers slipping beneath the cloth to tug at the elastic briefs. "I like these shorts. When you bend over—"

Kim sealed his words with her kiss. Locking her palms to the rugged contours of his jaw, she fitted her lips to his.

Nick's arms tightened, his indrawn breath lifting his broad chest against her breasts. His left hand stroked the length of her back slowly, easing beneath her T-shirt to rest low on her spine. His right hand cupped the back of her head, pressuring her to his seeking mouth.

He tasted . . . hungry.

She wanted to be nearer him, to feel his hard body

mold to her softer contours. His hands continued to stroke her lightly and Nick's breathing increased.

Kim began to tremble, her legs aching with tension. When his tongue traced her mouth, she groaned, feeling him harden beneath her hips. She felt herself falling into a sensuous pool, rippling with the need for ultimate fulfillment.

Nick's tall body went hard as his kiss eased. "Oh, Lord. I want you, too, honey," he rumbled unevenly as he stroked her back and hips. "I hurt with it. But we could have visitors at any time."

He kissed her lightly, staring into her eyes. "You ignite me, Kim. I feel like I'm shooting into flames when we're like this."

Aching with her need for him, Kim closed her eyes. "I can't afford you, Nick. I just can't."

"Do you like kissing my daddy?" Cherry asked almost clinically. Seated cross-legged next to them, she held her puppy in her arms. Glancing at her red plastic wristwatch, she announced, "Fletch showed me how to use my stop watch. I'm going to start timing your smooches. Kim's good to kiss, isn't she, Daddy? She smells good, and she's warm and soft. She hugs good, too."

"I was enjoying kissing her—past tense." Groaning, Nick eased Kim to lie beside him, her head resting on his shoulder.

Cherry immediately occupied his other arm and looked across his bare chest to Kim. She winked just as the puppy romped across Nick's flat stomach, leaping over Kim. "Daddy's big enough for both of us, Kimmy." She placed her pudgy hand on Nick's stubbled cheek and tugged his mouth to hers for a kiss. "Do I get to keep my puppy, Daddy?"

He grinned, ruffling her curls. "Okay. I didn't stand a chance between you two. What kind of odds did you make on me agreeing to the puppy?"

"Two to one. There's two of us now and just one of you. It's neat having Kimmy for a mommy," Cherry stated thoughtfully. Her eyes widened. "I know, Daddy. I'm too little, but if you'd let Kimmy sleep with you, I bet *she* could keep the bad dreams away."

Nick's arms tightened about Kim's waist, his gaze hot and raking. It did nothing to stabilize her aching need. "She's sure as hell welcome to try, Cherry."

CHAPTER SEVEN

THAT EVENING, KIM placed chips on the roulette table. Stunned by Nick's meaningful stares throughout the day, she played carelessly.

"What's the matter, beautiful?" Duke asked her quietly. "You look like somebody's stepped on your pretty little toes."

Kim didn't feel the need to pretend with the big Texan. "Your friend—"

"*Your* husband, Kim," Duke interrupted with a wide grin. "He's like concentrated hootch, isn't he? Something's got the big galoot on tenterhooks. Offhand, I'd say that something was you."

Kim placed another bet—and lost again. "Are you sure it isn't his ex-wife?" she asked glumly. Nick made her feel . . . stalked. As if she walked a fraying tightrope high in the sky while he waited for her with open arms on the ground below. She wasn't used to playing sensual games, and she was all too aware that Nick knew all the rules.

"Uh-uh, honey chil'. Nick stays cool under fire. I've seen it in Nam, and I've seen it in the past when that . . . witch starts acting up. Something else has set fire to his tail feathers. How about having a drink with me? I'm a good listener."

"I'll bet you are, but I'm on duty now. Thanks for

asking, though." Kim saw a small ancient woman hit Fletch with her purse. "Excuse me. Duty calls."

Duke's hand snagged her forearm lightly, his tanned face concerned as he looked down at her. "Honey, if you need a friend, I can be a pretty good one. Remember that."

"Okay," Kim agreed slowly. "I will."

The eighty-year-old woman had backed Fletch into a corner when Kim asked solicitously, "Is he picking on you?"

The woman swung her huge purse at the ex-boxer one last time and blurted out, "This ape accused me of palming cards. My great grandchildren have better sense than he has."

Fletch's massive face dropped. "Uh, she's got aces rubber-banded to her arm, Kim. I saw her."

The grandmother took a deep indignant breath, swinging her purse another time. "Damn you, sonny."

Kim touched her shoulder lightly. "He thinks he's doing his job. Sometimes he's a little too zealous. Would you like to report him to his boss?"

When confronted, the woman's wrinkles shifted into a crafty expression. "Nicky Santos?"

When Kim nodded, the woman grinned. "He's a nice boy. Sure, I'll talk to him. Without you."

"Nick always gives her handouts. That's why she didn't want you with her. He's a fall guy for sob stories," Fletch grumbled as the elderly lady wove a wobbly trail toward Nick's office.

Five minutes later the office door opened and the elderly woman shot a victorious look at Fletch and lifted a handful of green bills and waved them at him before leaving the casino.

"See? Nick's a softy and everyone knows it," the ex-boxer said before he lumbered into the crowd.

Duke waved at Kim walking past Fletch toward her. "Green silk is a beautiful color on you, Kim. Ready for a break, baby doll?" he asked.

She smiled. "Thank you. You're a kind soul, Duke. I'd love to get off my feet for a few moments."

"Great. I've got a lot of time to kill. My oil-well buyer has a big gambling appetite. He aims to be here all night and morning. I have to be around to tuck him in and fly him back to Texas in a few days to sober up." The flat of his hand on her back lightly guided Kim through the casino to a booth in a darkened lounge.

When they'd settled into it, the waitress placed a bourbon and water in front of Duke and served Kim hot herbal tea.

"So how's married life, little lady?" The Texan's eyebrows lifted. "And don't feed me any hogwash either."

Kim traced the rim of her cup with her forefinger. She liked Duke, sensing that behind his twinkling green eyes lurked a sensitive man. She smiled. "We're just going through an adjustment, Duke. It's nothing serious."

"Serious, hell. Nick looks like he'd like to break things and you look white as a ghost. You need to relax, lady. Tell old dad all about it," Duke drawled.

"You Texans probably hear as slow as you talk," Kim teased. "But you're right. I could use a little relaxation."

"See? Old dad was right. Nick's got a meeting with the chamber of commerce tomorrow afternoon. He won't mind if we play golf or tennis."

Kim thought about Nick's anger and frustration when she'd driven his Porsche. "Could you teach me to drive a stick shift better, Duke?"

"Sure as hell could, honey. I once had a girl friend who raced in the Grand Prix." He frowned, staring over Kim's shoulder. "Great Elmo's guts! Nick's coming this way and he looks—"

Kim followed Duke's stare. Shouldering through the crowd, Nick looked awesome, his expression fierce. When he reached their booth, he wrapped his fingers about Kim's upper arm and hauled her up beside him. "I lost you," he rapped out bluntly, staring at Duke, then at Kim.

She didn't like the accusation glittering in his single eye. Nor did she like being handled like an errant child. "Now you've found me. I can take my breaks, can't I, boss?" she asked, daring him to answer.

Duke glanced at the tight wrap of Nick's fingers about her arm. "Lighten up, buddy."

"She's *my* wife, Duke. You've got the field. Go play it," Nick snapped.

"He's your friend," Kim declared later. "You're acting jealous, Nick Santos. Right up to your eye patch," she accused from her side of the Porsche as it slid into the garage at two o'clock the next morning.

"So he's my friend. He's also the fastest Romeo in town." Nick grasped her left hand and the huge ruby ring caught fire from the overhead lights. "This says it—married."

Sliding her hand from his, Kim took a deep breath. "You mean bought and paid for, Nick. Temporarily. I don't like your attitude. Duke is a friend."

"Don't you understand, Kim?" Nick hit the flat of his hand against the steering wheel. "I want every part of you."

The small enclosure of the car intensified the angles and planes of Nick's rugged face and the hard set of his jaw. "Damn you, woman," he growled. "Can't you see? I love you. We could make this marriage work. Really work."

Kim somehow unlatched the car door and stood on shaky knees. She needed the sanctuary of her room desperately. "I hate it when you push, Nick. Nothing could work under those circumstances. I'm used to dealing on my terms, not someone else's."

"You're used to closing people off. I just told you I loved you and you turned white. Dammit, I'm going to find out why," he stated flatly as he slammed the car door shut. "Life comes around one time, sweetheart, and you're too good to let get away. Duke's off limits as of now!"

"Don't tell me what to do, Nick Santos!" Kim shouted across the car at him. "I can choose my own friends." What was it about the arrogant, possessive man that could shatter her intentions to remain cool and in control?

"I suppose you're headed for your fortress—that damned bedroom," Nick growled. "I never thought my woman would hide from reality—"

"Ooooo . . ." Kim groaned, throwing up her hands. "You're impossible. And I'm too tired to deal with you. Just let me have some peace," she ordered, stalking toward the front door of the hacienda.

When he opened the door, Kim marched past him. As she closed her bedroom door, Nick's quiet voice halted her. "Let me know when you find that peace."

Kim finally slid into bed, his words "I love you" echoing into the darkness.

Two hours later, she opened his bedroom door, drawn by the sounds of his nightmares. In the shadows, the room looked as bad as the noise entering her bedroom had indicated. Gathering her terry-cloth robe around her, she asked, "Nick? Are you all right?"

He blinked owlishly against the hallway light slicing into his dark bedroom. His hair stood out in peaks and he shoved his hand through the curls. The white satin sheet slithered down to his hips, baring his chest as he sat up. Breathing rapidly, he peered at her, and Kim knew he fought the nightmare chasing him. "I'm here, Nick. It's Kim."

His powerful chest tightened, his hands gripping the sheet as if he could tear it. "You're dreaming, Nick," she continued softly, approaching the round water bed. His expression was that of shattering fear, a silent plea.

Kim felt as if invisible fingers squeezed her heart. When she reached to touch his shoulder, it was damp with perspiration. Soothingly, she stroked across the brawny planes of his back, waiting. Gradually, Nick's torn expression eased and he flung himself back against the pillows, his forearm covering his eyes. In a ragged, disgusted timbre, he cursed, "Hell! I woke you up."

He breathed heavily and Kim sat down, watching him, wanting to wrap him in her arms. She couldn't resist stroking his hair and temples. Every particle in her told her to comfort him, to understand his pain. "Everyone else is asleep, darling. Can I get you something?"

His hand caught hers, bringing it to his mouth. "You, lady. You're all I want. Sleep with me."

The desperation and force tangled in his voice plunged into Kim. "I can't, Nick. I—"

"Sleep with me, Kim. That's all I meant. Be my security blanket for the night," Nick stated roughly as if asking her chipped at his pride. "Believe it or not, I've never made that offer in my life, woman." His voice sharpened. "Hell! You just went white again. Can't you trust me just for tonight?"

His strong fingers locked with hers and she felt the dampness of his palm. "I need a friend in the night, sweetheart," he whispered in a raspy tone that tore holes in Kim's control. "Come on." He lifted the sheet as an invitation, tugging her hand toward him. "I'm decent. For once, I've got pajama bottoms on."

"I get the feeling I'm going to be sorry for this," Kim murmured as she slipped between the sheets.

"I won't be," he sighed as he wrapped his arms around her and drew her into the cove of his lap. "Wake me if I start thrashing around. I don't want to hurt you."

The night was a long and restless one for Kim. And as morning light filled the room, she resented Nick's easy sprawl across the entire water bed; he'd slept like a baby while she barely dozed.

* * *

It was early afternoon when Kim downshifted Duke's customized Rolls, preparing for the curve. Duke's big hand rested on her shoulder, patting her as she shifted back up into third gear. "Great going, girl. Nothing to it, huh?"

"You should have seen when Nick was instructing me. He has no patience at all. He acted like I was actually trying to destroy his baby," Kim said, downshifting confidently for a stoplight. She liked the easy way the Texan lounged back in the cushioned upholstery. "You're not afraid of my driving, are you?"

"Nope. Relaxed as a limp flag up a pole." Duke sighed deeply. "In fact, you could apply for the job as my chauffeur." He paused, then said, "It's really true, Kim. The ones closest to you don't make good driving teachers."

"I can't imagine Nick teaching anything. He's not a patient man." Kim laughed, slightly inebriated by her increased driving skills. The hood's longhorns swooped down the highway, the big car obeying her touch. "Don't get any ideas about me chauffeuring you anywhere. Once this job is finished, I'm not working for another man. They're too contrary."

"Job?" Duke asked sharply. Kim had forgotten the keen mind behind the Texan's easygoing facade, and now regretted the slip of her tongue. "Job," he repeated slowly, his green eyes tracing her profile in the afternoon sun. "Great balls of fire, that's it." He snapped his fingers. "I knew something didn't sit right, honey chil'. I've known Nick too long. Even he'd take more time choosing a bride. He'd have you hog-tied in a Jamaican cabana longer than a week, Kim. Or on a love boat for two. Shoot! That's it!" He snapped his fingers again. "Nick's got you and you won't let him wind you around his little pinky like the rest of his women. That's what's driving him down the jealousy road. I'll be damned. Nick's playing a scam that's backfiring on him. You're the pretty little fly in Laura's ointment, aren't you? That's a damned smart idea!"

Kim clutched the leather grooves of the steering wheel. She liked the big Texan, but could she trust him? She slanted him a glance, reading the excitement in his expression. "You'll have to talk to Nick about any big ideas you're tossing around beneath your sombrero, cowboy."

Duke's fingers caressed her bare shoulder lightly. "I like that. A woman who defers to her man and master," he teased.

"Nick would like it, too." Kim laughed, suddenly feeling freed of her burden. It was good to have the Texan as a friend.

He drew a small circle on her skin, idly watching the desert browns and blue grays fly by the Rolls's window. On an impulse, Kim asked, "Have you slept with every woman you've known, Duke? Nick says you have."

She giggled when he blushed. "Not quite. But I've tried," he admitted boldly. "It would be different with you."

Suddenly, Kim felt her lighthearted mood dissolve. "I'm not in the market, Duke."

His face was serious when he turned to her. "The way I see it, I'll wait around. Unless things change, either you or Nick is going to need someone to pick up the pieces."

Nick stared out of the chamber of commerce board room, barely alert to the topic of the early afternoon meeting, "Beautification of Las Vegas Streets." Lost in his private thoughts, he rubbed his thigh, remembering Kim's concerned expression as she'd massaged the pain.

Kim. Wrapped by bonds Nick didn't understand, she danced through his mind, tormenting him. Not really seeing the flow of traffic beyond the window, Nick thought about Kim. What pain had she known? She was wary, frightened of her own emotions when they burst through her reserve. She'd acted as if he'd slapped her when he told her he loved her. Why?

A familiar sight—a steel-colored Rolls with long-horns attached to its hood—stopped for a traffic light. Nick sat up, catching a glimpse of Duke's big Stetson on the passenger side. The Rolls turned right onto a side street and Kim's flaxen ponytail shone in the afternoon sun. He'd recognize the proud lift of her chin within a mile.

"Damn!" Nick cursed, standing and packing his briefcase quickly.

The chamber president's head swiveled toward him. "What's wrong, Nick?"

"I've just remembered something I have to take care of, Clyde. It can't wait . . . I'll call you later." Nick strode toward the exit.

"Kim," he roared, damning the forty-five minutes it took him to get out of the crowded parking lot and drive to the ranchette. He slammed the door of the ranch house behind him. "Where are you?"

She rounded the hallway, dressed in her jogging shorts and a T-shirt that read, "Health Nut," glaring at him over Cherry's sleeping, tear-stained face. Shifting his daughter higher on her hip, Kim asked too softly, "You called . . . oh, Great One?"

Nick felt as if he'd been punched in the gut. "What happened?" he whispered, easing his arm beneath Cherry and taking her weight against him.

Kim's blue eyes flashed fire up at him, her fists locking into her waist. "Laura called and talked to Cherry . . . Maria had just calmed her down when I got here. Your mother's exhausted—she's resting, Nick. Laura told Cherry that she's taking her away and Cherry locked herself in the bathroom. Your ex-wife is a real sweetheart, Nick. Cherry's scared to death."

"I see," he said quietly, feeling all the anger and jealousy drain out of him. Cherry issued a shuddering last sigh and nestled against his chest, her thumb half out of her mouth.

"Laura must not talk to Cherry without one of us in attendance, Nick. I forbid it," Kim ordered, stalking the length of the sunken living room.

Nick nodded slowly. "I agree. I didn't really think she'd contact Cherry without going through the formalities. She has no right for visitation."

Kim faced him. "Laura is cruel, Nick. She'd destroy Cherry in a minute. We have to protect her."

For a moment, Nick absorbed her rage, watching her stride across the room. Laura hadn't a chance. Kim knew the odds now and she was gearing up for a battle royal to defend his daughter. His heart began to pound against his chest. Kim was one hundred and twenty pounds of passionate, fighting, loving woman, true to her obligations. She didn't know it yet, but one day she'd fight that hard for him, he vowed.

"We can handle the situation . . . together," he said, easing down onto the sofa to cradle his daughter.

"That woman's a real pain in the—" Kim's tawny eyebrows lifted and her hand covered her mouth as if she just realized her words. "Nick Santos, if you laugh at me, I'll deck you," she promised hotly.

Nick wanted her *on* the deck. Beneath him. Aroused.

"Lucky lady, no one's laughing. I'm just pleased to know that Cherry can count on you."

"I'm mad, Nick. Don't try to pacify me." Kim knelt by Cherry and smoothed her damp hair back from her forehead. "Poor baby. She's cried herself to sleep."

Nick couldn't help it. He reached out, cupping the back of Kim's head to draw her to him. He kissed her nose, felt her breath sweep across his lips before his mouth caressed hers tenderly. "You're my woman, lady. A hell of a woman."

Against his lips, she whispered unevenly, "I'm not used to worrying about other people . . ."

Keep a light touch, Nick reminded himself. Kim's

beautiful eyes were damp now, her gaze searching his. "It hurts, Nick. To see her cry," she whispered in a voice that tore at his heart.

Her fingers crept slowly between his and inwardly, Nick sighed.

He loved her.

When her eyes darkened, he realized he'd spoken aloud.

"No, Nick. Don't—" she gasped, withdrawing from his touch.

It was the single time in Cherry's brief life that Nick regretted holding his daughter. He wanted to comfort Kim. Something like fear roamed her expression, freezing upon her beautiful face and chilling his bones. "No," she repeated. "You just want me. I'm a challenge to you."

"That, too," Nick managed to say, his throat raw with emotion. Damn, where had he gone wrong? Kim appeared unnerved, her fingers wringing against each other.

"We've both just been worried about Cherry—" she began logically, staring at him wild-eyed, her face pale in its frame of curling wisps.

Nick yearned to cradle her, to smooth whatever fears chased her. "Lean on me, Kim. Trust me . . ." God, he'd love the woman until she was a hundred . . . longer.

She stood gracefully, her body a fluid dance of muscle and bone. "You demand too much, Nick. Too much. I can't risk it."

Can't risk it. The phrase danced on the tension in the room like a live snake over hot coals. Why? he wondered once more.

"Don't bet on it, sweetheart," he responded more quietly than he felt. "I'm used to getting what I want."

After the silence at Maria's dinner table, Nick leaned against the wall of the workout room. He sipped iced bourbon and cola, watching Kim throw herself into aerobics. The hard beat of "Rocky" throbbed from her portable stereo as Kim's lithe body contorted rhythmically in front of the mirrors lining the wall.

He knew Kim threw herself into the music with every ounce of strength she possessed. She reminded him of a beautiful wild butterfly trying to escape a net. He watched her grow tired, her movements slowing, perspiration trailing from her pink sweatband and onto the matching leotard, darkening it between her breasts.

"Okay, Kim. That's enough," he ordered, stalking toward the tape deck to click it off. He sat his glass on the workout mat. "I'm not going to let you kill yourself."

She rounded on him in a fury. "You know it all, don't you?" she accused before he lashed her to him solidly.

"I know you've been going at this for two straight hours. That's enough. I'm here now. Take whatever is bothering you out on me, Kim. Come on, let's have it."

She struggled against him, frustration shimmering in her cerulean blue eyes. "Oh, I'd like to. I'd really like to, Nick."

"It will work out, honey," he soothed. "We weren't ready for Laura's claws. But we'll be ready next time. Cherry will be just fine." He wanted her teasing him, calling him "mean old thing," laughing at him. He tried to smile at her furious face. "Hey. We could skip work tonight and go to an auction for movie star memorabilia. It's a charity thing."

Kim's bottom lip pouted and Nick forced himself not to taste it. "I don't like being manipulated, Nick. You don't have to pacify me."

"Who's manipulating you? Mom will see to it that Laura doesn't contact Cherry again, and I've been wanting to go to the benefit," he said innocently. "You're a fan of old movies; you'll enjoy it."

* * *

In their kitchen later, draped in a Mae West boa, Kim relaxed, laughing at Nick's attempts to swallow a quick-energy shake containing two raw eggs. He licked the malt coating from his upper lip, enjoying her rich, husky laughter. To hear her laugh was worth drinking anything.

Kim didn't move her hand when he held it, sipping the bland concoction. "Are you going to sleep with me tonight, Kim?" he asked softly over the slow thud of his own heart. "To keep the bogeyman away?"

"Mean old thing," she teased laughingly, and Nick relaxed slightly, loving the growing intimacy between them. "You're pushing again," she reminded him gently.

"I can't stop, honey," he admitted ruefully.

"I know. You're programmed to get your way." She slipped her hand from his, her face averted. "Thank you for the wonderful time, Nick. I really enjoyed myself tonight."

CHAPTER EIGHT

"LAURA AND CHARLES are parked in our living room, Kim," Nick announced the next morning. "They were driving by and just thought they'd pop in. Thank God, Mom took Cherry grocery shopping this morning," he rapped out after he'd clicked off the hard beat of her stereo, catching her at the height of her workout.

Poised in mid-exercise, Kim's palms were flat on the mat, her bottom high in the air, facing Nick. She stared at him through her braced, spread legs. He didn't look as formidable as he had the previous night.

Even upside down, though, Nick looked ruggedly handsome. Dressed in worn blue jeans and a navy polo shirt, he was barefoot, holding his morning coffee cup. A chewed-up morning paper was tucked under his muscular arm. His hair was rumpled and his stubble-covered cheek bore sleep marks. He looked endearing. Mr. Ordinary House Husband, U.S.A.

The novelty of the thought locked Kim's palms to the mat and she continued studying his inverted image.

Freed of the gambler image he portrayed at the casino, Nick looked . . . lovable, she decided. His hair was a little too long, curling low on his collar, and his polo shirt was unbuttoned to reveal his hair-covered chest. It was a nice chest, actually, with two flat brown nipples centered in rippling pectoral muscles. He had called them his erogenous zones.

"You invited the witch," he accused moodily, rubbing his right thigh. "She's got her banker in tow." He grimaced, taking the tattered newspaper from beneath his arm to stare at it moodily. *"Lassie* is happy anyway. He's found my shoes. He's either wet on them or chewed them."

"You poor baby," Kim soothed teasingly, unable to still her smile.

"Are you being deliberately provocative, Kim?" Nick accused after a short silence in which he stared at her curiously, his gaze smoldering over her hips and thighs. "The view is definitely enticing, Mrs. Santos. Gravity is doing interesting things to your...ah...chest."

The intimate-sounding raspy voice swept over Kim, heating her inwardly. The workout had made her feel good, alert, and in charge after a sleepless night. *He*, for once, looked at the disadvantage. Without her usual control, Kim giggled as she straightened, stretching. "You're not so bad yourself, Mr. Santos."

Nick's gaze was steamy and sultry. It traveled over her tight black leotard with microscopic intensity, probing the rapid rise and fall of her breasts. "You're feeling on top of it, lady."

She patted the corner of her towel across her face, then draped it protectively around her neck, covering her breasts. Her nipples had hardened under his gaze ...in fact, every molecule of her body seemed to do its own special aerobics when Nick came close. "I always do after a workout. It's a natural high for me."

"Hmmm," he rumbled speculatively. "I'll remember that. I could use a good workout and a natural high myself," he drawled in a tone that caressed her. He sighed, his mouth firming. "But for now, Laura and Charles..."

"I'll make coffee, Nick."

"I've already jumped Laura about talking to Cherry

that way. You don't have to do a thing for those vipers." He frowned, the crease between his eyebrows deepening as she patted his cheek lightly.

"Now, Nick. Be polite. They're guests in our home," she said sweetly.

He blinked. "You're not for real, lady."

"You catch more flies with honey, Nick . . ."

Dressed in a light blue linen suit that smacked of French design, Laura stalked the living room, smoking a slim cheroot. Charles was dowdy, balding, and overweight in his gray business suit.

Laura pivoted when Kim entered the living room with a coffee tray. Her blue eyes slashed icily at Nick as he took the tray from Kim to place it on a low table. "How domestic. Ma and Pa Kettle on the farm," she remarked sharply. "Nick, she looks positively . . . sweaty."

"I *am* sweaty, Laura. I've been working out. You could use a little muscle tone, too," Kim said easily. She was determined not to let the other woman place her at the disadvantage in her own home. "We haven't had our morning coffee yet. Would you like a cup?" Without waiting for a reply, she poured four cups of coffee and handed one to Charles with a smile. "We've never met, Charles. I'm Kim Santos."

Ignoring her pleasantries, Charles helped himself to two teaspoons of sugar. "Let's get to it, Laura. Let's make the arrangements and get back to New York." He attempted an intimidating glare at Nick. "I don't have much time to dilly-dally around. I'm a regular businessman. Banking, you know. And banking requires regular hours."

Sprawled against a corner of the couch, his left arm resting upon the back, Nick braced his long legs on a low table. He appeared to be comfortable, but Kim noted his right hand slowly traveling up and down his thigh. His long dark fingers trembled slightly, and she remembered his pain.

Her instincts told her to protect him *and* Cherry, to

create a believable scenario of their marriage. Holding her cup, Kim settled within the cove of his body. She placed her ankles lightly over his, letting her left hand settle over his muscular thigh. She stroked it in an obvious caress and felt the tension in his big body ease. She smiled up at him, ignoring the other couple. For good measure, she lifted her face to him and Nick immediately brushed her lips with his own.

The tenderness of his mouth upon hers jolted Kim, tingling after he'd lifted his head. Nick's dark stare down at her blazed with sensuality.

The gesture did as it was intended. Laura was livid, glaring at their relaxed pose. "We want Cherry. Name your price, Nick," she snarled. "You can't possibly want her intruding on your . . . new marriage."

Nick's fingers cupped Kim's shoulder tensely. "Cherry has no price, Laura. I have custody and I'm keeping it."

"Now, my good man—" Charles protested, but Laura interrupted him.

She pointed a finger at Kim. "I've had *her* investigated, Nick! She's not a fit mother and I can prove it. She ran off with her husband's money, but before that, when she was just a teenager, she had an abortion. She was married—if she'd wanted kids she would have had them. I'm warning you, Nick, the judge will take all that into account."

Nick's muscular body stiffened beside her and Kim forced herself to smile easily up at him. His grim expression leveled at Laura. "Come ahead. Try your damnedest," he challenged. "I've got a few things to say about you myself. Perhaps Charles would be interested right now."

"They'd be lies, Nick." But Laura flinched, going pale beneath her makeup.

"You had a string of affairs while we were married. Proof shouldn't be hard to get—"

"Nick!" Laura screamed, striding toward the door as

Charles followed her huffily. "You'll pay for this, so help me!"

Laura turned and threatened, "I'm going to get Cherry, Nick. Biological mothers have rights." She slammed the door behind them.

Kim stared at the closed door after they had gone, her hand still on his thigh. "She *is* a witch."

"Or worse," he remarked glumly, wrapping his large hand around her neck and easing her face toward his. "Are you going to tell me, Kim? Or let the investigators hit me with it in court? The abortion . . ." he prompted. His expression was wary and concerned. "Please trust me, Kim."

She fought the chill that invaded her bones each time she remembered her past life. She'd tied all the loneliness and pain into a neat bundle and hidden it away. Now, unless she opened up to Nick, her past could endanger Cherry.

Closing her eyes, and leaning back against his forearm, Kim began her story. "I didn't have an abortion. I miscarried the baby I'd wanted so desperately. Looking back, I realize I wanted her—her, my baby girl," she repeated, "to fill all the lonely places of my childhood. Her father, a boy my age—seventeen—was another of my struggles to find that love."

She shrugged, continuing. "I misconstrued his interest in sex as love and got pregnant. My parents were shocked as always by my behavior, never really understanding that they hadn't allowed me into their relationship. I was so lonely as a child. I'd lie in bed, listening to them laugh, just hoping one of them could spare a little time for me."

"When my mother died four years ago, my father looked up from her grave at me. There was no warmth, no love—I could have been a passing stranger. He's trapped by her memory. She's dead and there's still no room for me . . ."

Continuing, she felt as if she were a fragile piece of

china, cracking, giant pieces falling to the earth, shattering . . .

"Richard, my ex-husband, met all my parents' requirements. Maybe that's partly why I married him. I thought I loved him—I don't remember now. Children fitted his needs—as ornaments for an up-and-coming executive. I wanted them borne out of love. Somehow the love I felt for him when we married slipped away . . . I took only enough cash to begin a new life. I left everything else with him."

The warm glide of Nick's fingertip down her cheek brought her back to the present. She'd been crying and he traced her tears lightly.

Trying to stabilize the devastation within her, Kim wiped her eyes with the back of her hand. "I don't know why I'm crying. I'm sorry."

Nick rocked her in his arms. "Don't be. But I'm glad you trusted me enough to tell me. I understand a lot of things about you now. Like the loving way you take to Cherry, as if she were your own daughter," he whispered huskily against her temple.

Through her tears, Kim stared up at his concerned frown. She traced the heavy line of his brows. "Don't look so worried, Nick. I couldn't stand it either if anything happened to Cherry."

"Nothing is going to happen to Cherry, not with my tigress around," he said roughly. "I'm the only one who knows the whole story about you, aren't I? I feel like you've given me a very precious gift, Kim."

The tenderness written in his whisker-stubbled face shot through her, melting her caution. She had no choice but to lock her arms around his neck, holding him with all her might. Nick hugged her tightly, securely, until her heartbeat slowed. She felt the warm déjà vu wash over her once more—*Coming home.*

He eased her face from the cove of his neck and shoulder, tipping her chin up with his knuckle. "Hey! What's all this? You could go to a guy's head, lady." He grinned, brushing his lips over hers. "Any old port in the storm?"

Nick—warm, rumpled, and lovable—was suddenly an intimate part of her life. She trusted him explicitly and couldn't resist teasing him. "Mean old thing."

His grin widened. "That endearment isn't much. I get revved up every time you throw it at me, wanting to disprove your theory. But it's a start, lady mine."

Kim couldn't resist snuggling down on his chest, safe and warm within his arms. She sighed, noting how very comfortable he was to cuddle. The easy rise and fall of his chest felt good against her cheek; his hand stroking her back gently. "Thank you, Nick. For listening."

"Any time, Mrs. Santos." His arms tightened. "Do I get a kiss for being Mr. Nice Guy?"

"Opportunist," she accused with a smile.

"Damn right I am." The kiss began as a tender exploration, but it blazed into wildfire, and somehow Kim lay beneath Nick on the couch, his hand cupping her breast. His mouth was urgent upon hers, the weight of his body pressing her down into the cushions. Arching against him, Kim's legs tangled with his long ones, the melting core of her needing his fulfillment. Beneath her palm, his back rippled as he gathered her closer . . . closer, his blatant hardness thrusting against her abdomen. His lips caressed her hot cheek, his beard slightly chafing her skin.

When his fingers sought and found the delicacy of her nipple, Kim shot into flames, her legs twisting about his. She shuddered, her fingers slipping beneath his belt, low on his spine.

She wanted him totally.

Lifting her hips against his hardness, Kim felt the trembling sweep of his large hands over her, the harshness of his breath against her cheek.

She barely heard the two car doors close beyond the house as Nick's mouth settled on hers. Cradling his jaw, Kim urged him from her. The blatant passion coloring his cheeks and smoldering in his eye questioned her. "Nick, someone just pulled up in the driveway."

For a moment he stared at her, not comprehending. Then his eye closed and he shuddered, allowing his head to rest on her breast for a moment. He nuzzled the softness and groaned. "I get no respect," he said with a wry half smile as he sat up.

Aching from the loss of his warm body against hers, Kim shared his regret. She eased upward and drew a cushion against her. Nick drew a line down her hot cheek. "Hot stuff," he teased.

"Speak for yourself, mean old thing," Kim returned with a tremulous smile.

"Kim! Daddy!" Cherry called just beyond the living-room door. "Me and Nana are home."

"Just in time," Nick drawled, lacing his fingers with Kim's shaking ones.

Early that evening Nick watched Kim coolly maneuver a drunken woman out of the casino. Dressed in a sleek black dress supported by thin straps, her hair piled into a tousled mass on top of her head, Kim appeared to have recovered her control.

Nick's stare drifted down over her full curves as he thought about the morning. Kim had been stunned by their lovemaking. "Oh, Nick . . ." she'd stammered, her fingers shaking as they covered her kiss-swollen mouth.

Hell, he thought, she probably *was* devastated. They'd been caught like two hungry teenagers in the back seat of a car. He ached now, his loins throbbing. He wanted a double whiskey, straight up. No, he corrected. He wanted Kim hungry, beneath him, her deep-throated purrs sending him into the warm, sweet luxury of her body.

"Hi, honey." A tall showgirl, dressed in bits of plumes and sequins, coiled herself around him, and out of habit Nick placed his hand on her bare waist. "Lonesome tonight, Nick? I hear married life can get a little old."

"I've only been married a week and a half, Shawnee. Give me a chance," Nick responded with a wry smile.

Shawnee's long red nails prowled the front of his tuxedo. "Yeah, well. Remember me when things get cold, huh?"

Nick barely heard her. Across the crowded casino, Kim stared at him, her blue eyes blazing at the showgirl coiled around him. "Shawnee, get lost," Nick ordered, watching Kim's chin harden. Then all of a sudden, she smiled. Coldly.

Damn, he thought, starting toward her. She was just looking for an excuse to backtrack on their growing relationship. He'd come too close to the real Kim and it had frightened her.

By the time he shouldered through the crowd, Kim was deep into an animated conversation with Duke. Nick felt a shaft of fear slice through him as she looked up at his face. Her expression was a mixture of livid anger and cool disguise. The bright blue eyes lashed at him, though her mouth smiled.

"I want to talk to you, Kim," Nick rasped, ignoring Duke. "Now."

God, he was scared. Kim looked so distant . . . and so hurt.

"Trouble, buddy?" Duke asked lazily. "Can I help?"

Nick grabbed Kim's upper arm, tugging her toward his office. "Family business," he rapped out at Duke.

Once in the office, he wondered if he did need Duke's help. Locking the door behind him, he turned to her. Reaching for her, he said, "Kim, you can't be for real. Shawnee was just—"

Kim thrust both palms against his chest, stalking away from him. Turning, her body taut, she looked like a tigress ready to spring. "Don't you dare touch me, Nick Santos! You just crave every woman who comes near you, don't you? Well, not *this* one!"

When Nick moved toward her, wanting to soothe her, she jumped behind a chair and his heart plummeted down to the pit of his stomach. "Now, Kim. Shawnee is just a girl who works for me—"

"Like I do," she stated. "We're both just here for you to use, aren't we, Nick?"

Nick ran his fingers through his hair. She'd opened up to him this morning, given him insight into her loneliness. Where had all that gone? "It's been a hell of a day, Kim. I don't feel like fighting a jealous wife—"

"Me?" Her eyebrows lifted disbelievingly. "Me, jealous?" She shook her head vehemently and several of the curls tumbled to her shoulder. "I only work for you, lover boy."

"Lover boy?" he repeated slowly and Kim knew she'd cut the bare leash tethering Nick Santos. She hadn't meant to go that far and now she regretted calling him the name. He looked fierce and determined. His nostrils flared and the hardness of his mouth eased into a sensual line. "Honey, you've got a hot little temper when you get revved up. You're not exactly immune yourself. You practically asked for it this morning."

"You're not getting *it,* Santos! And I did *not* ask for anything this morning." She hated him. Nick made her feel primitive, the layers of her sophistication peeling off like dead skin. He made her feel hot *and* cold. She balled her hands into fists to keep from launching into him.

His teeth shone brightly against his dark skin. "You're a physical lady, despite the cool image you project to other people. Come here. I'll show you what to do with all that energy. You're wasting it on those exercises, when I'm aching for you."

"Nick!"

"In fact," he continued in a drawl as he loosened and stripped off his tie and discarded his jacket, "this room is soundproof, honey, and the door is locked."

Catching his meaning, Kim glanced at the long sumptuous couch. Nick flipped open the buttons of his shirt, sauntering toward her. "You started it, Goldilocks. You're not immune to me, sexually or otherwise. In fact, despite your efforts to cover up, you're a loving woman. As sweet and responsive as a man could want."

Taking a step backward, Kim felt the corner of the desk against her hips. She'd pushed him over the edge, and Nick looked bent on seduction. She knew if he touched her she'd ignite . . .

He threw his shirt onto the back of the chair and Kim stared with a dry throat at the width of his powerful chest, hair covering the tanned skin. She began to shake, her knees buckling as Nick's large hand covered her right breast in a barbaric demonstration of possession.

"You're mine," he spoke in a low purr that riveted her feet to the carpet. His long fingers splayed against the golden smoothness of her upper breast, caressing lightly as his palm heated the aching softness.

"I hadn't planned to make love with you here . . . but your jealousy of Shawnee . . ." He grinned rakishly. "Hell, a man likes to know his woman reacts the way you do. It lets him know just where you stand."

"I didn't mean—" She braced her hands on the desk, bending backward as Nick leaned toward her.

He smiled—a tender, knowing smile. "Such big blue eyes . . . Afraid now, little witch? Don't be. You're like a live wire when I touch you. Come here," Nick taunted softly.

His male challenge ran over her like liquid fire. She stared at him helplessly, wanting to move into the warmth of his arms, barely tethering her desire.

Nick's fingers circled her wrists, drawing the left one to his lips. He placed her right palm over his chest and the heavy thud of his heart pounded into her palm. Unwillingly, Kim's fingers smoothed the steely texture. Holding her gaze, he traced the blue veins of her wrist with his mouth. "I need you, lover. Warm me with your love."

"Lover," she repeated in a whisper, conjuring his urgent body locked with hers. Kim felt the hard thrust of his maleness against her belly, the heat of his thighs warming hers. Nick was the personification of male sensuality, concentrated into a fever that ran hot through her veins. He needed her not only as a lover, but as a friend in the night. Her resistance to him was no stronger than a small spider's web.

"You're mine, honey," he whispered, slipping his fingers into the soft fall of her hair and tilting her face up to his. "My woman, my love. A part of me."

"Nick—" She was trembling, her blood seeming to run hot and cold, her heart beating wildly against her ribs. Already, her softness melded, flowed into the hard planes of his tall body.

"I need you like I need air," he whispered roughly before his mouth locked to hers.

She *did* ignite when he kissed her. Opening her mouth to his, Kim met his hunger with her own. Nick's big body tensed, his arms tightening, moving about her, cupping her hips with his hands and lifting her to his hardness. His groan stoked her hunger, her fingers sweeping through his curls, urging his mouth down upon hers.

Trembling, Nick gathered her closer, his large hands smoothing her hips restlessly, his breathing ragged. "God, you're sweet, lady love. Hot *and* sweet—"

Stroking his chest, tracing the rippling muscles of his quivering flat stomach, Kim *had* to seek his nipple with her mouth.

His sharply indrawn breath preceding his aching groan, "Kim . . . honey . . . you're rushing . . . I wanted to go so slow with you our first time . . ."

Brushing her lips against the hard planes of his chest, Kim barely heard the phone ring. Nick cupped her flushed face between his hands and pressed a rough, quick kiss on her parted lips.

"Damn, I'd like to tear the thing out of the wall," he muttered, smoothing her temples with his thumbs as he stared down at her. He shook her gently. "You're an explosive little package, wife. But I think we've picked the wrong time . . ."

Dazed, hungry, and aching for his mouth, Kim heard the phone ring again. Reality was the casino's office and the tender knowing smile written across Nick's rugged face.

Kim felt the heat of passion ooze from her. Shivering, feeling the aftershock of Nick's lovemaking down to her toenails, she edged from his body as the phone rang once more. He traced her upturned face, his expression darkening with frustration. "They wouldn't put the call through unless it was important, Kim," he said huskily.

His expression hardened. "Damn. You're afraid of yourself, not me, lady. You're afraid you're going to unlock all that and turn it loose. Whatever happened between you and your ex-husband isn't the same thing with you and me—I can feel it. You skid around commitments and emotions like a frightened child."

When she slid away from him, Nick growled, "Someday, little girl, there won't be an interruption to save you. Until then, you'd better walk on the light side of me," he ordered sharply. "I'm not used to being torn in two. Yes?" he snapped into the telephone. His scowl deepened as he listened and Kim wrapped her arms about herself to stop the waves of trembling washing over her.

"Cherry has run away." Nick's voice shook as he hung up the phone. "Mom said she was playing in front of Tammy's house when Laura pulled up and tried to get her into the car. Cherry ran into the desert, Kim. They haven't been able to find her."

Nick was pale and Kim knew what he was thinking —at eight o'clock the chilling desert was endless and dry, the coyotes foraging . . . "Let's go, Nick," Kim said softly, reaching for his discarded shirt. "I'll help you find her."

He stared at her upturned face, cradling it with his palm. He shook his head, attempting a smile. "I know you're not going to like this, lady, but you're one hell of a broad. Another woman might have turned tail just now, running from me. But you...well, like I said, you're one hell of a broad."

Half an hour later, the headlights of her Ford lifted and fell each time it hit a chuckhole. Driving slowly, Kim glanced at Nick's taut face as he flashed the spotlight over the sagebrush. "We'll find her, Nick."

"Yeah," he answered flatly. "It's cold out here. Cherry doesn't like to be cold."

Comforting him, Kim laced her fingers with his momentarily. He jerked his hand from her. "Keep your hands on the steering wheel, woman! We could hit a hole."

"Maybe in your low-slung Porsche. My car has more clearance," she said evenly, recognizing his tension.

Nick continued to flash the spotlight over the rugged terrain with his right hand. But his left palm locked to her knee, needing the physical reassurance of touch.

Two hours later—at eleven o'clock—he tensed forward in the seat. "Hey! What's that over there?" He shone the spotlight toward a clump of sagebrush. Cherry stepped into the blinding light.

Just after midnight, Nick leaned against the bathroom doorway sipping his third whiskey. He watched Kim kneel beside the tub. She playfully splashed bath water on Cherry, working to gently untangle the mop of dirtied curls. "It's all right, baby," Kim crooned, wiping Cherry's tear-stained face with a hand towel. "No one is taking you anywhere. Your daddy and I won't let them."

Maria came to the bathroom door, shaking her head and leaning against the other side of the doorway. "I'm too old for this, Nick. You make this marriage work. We need that girl around here." She smiled at Kim. "Thanks for helping, Kim. I'm glad you're here." She sighed. "I'll see you two in the morning. Good night."

"Good night, Maria. Sleep well," Kim responded as she helped Cherry out and wrapped her in a towel. "Nana's going to bed, Cherry. Are you sleepy, too?"

Exhausted, Cherry wrapped her arms about Kim's neck and nodded. "Sleep with me, Kimmy."

"Okay, Cherry, for a while. But then I've got to take a bath, too." Kim kissed her on the lips and hugged her. "You just remember what I said, darling. Your daddy and I won't let anyone take you away. We love you too much."

"I love you, Kimmy. And Daddy says you're one hell of a broad."

Nick stepped aside as she carried Cherry from the bathroom. His hand wrapped about her upper arm, staying her. The dimmed lights of the hallway exposed the dark circle under his eye, the heavy blue-black beard covering his hard jaw.

Cherry's chubby finger stroked Nick's lashes, and, round-eyed, she looked at Kim. "Daddy's crying. He's scared like I was. Will you take care of him, too?"

When Nick started to speak, he couldn't. Kim understood: Tough, determined Nick Santos was too full of emotion to speak. Once more, Kim responded to his need on a primitive instinct. She lifted her mouth to his, kissing him lightly.

"Thank you, Kim. For everything," he managed to say huskily, his fingers slipping from her arm reluctantly.

"I love her, too, Nick," Kim stated simply, shifting Cherry's weight in her arms. "You've been rubbing your leg. It's hurting, isn't it?"

He abruptly downed the last of the whiskey. "It's been a long day, Kim. You need to rest—not to worry about me."

Soaking in her bath later, Kim leaned back against the marble tile, closing her eyes. Nick had looked every minute of his forty-five years tonight. His loneliness had made her want to hold him, to cuddle him as she had Cherry. In contradiction to that feeling, she also wanted to nestle in the warmth of his strong arms. For tonight, she decided, she needed him as much as he needed her.

CHAPTER NINE

FRESH FROM HER bath, Kim slowly opened Nick's bedroom door. Dressed in a pink lacy teddy, covered by her short white terry-cloth robe, she had prepared well for the seduction of Nicholas "Accessible" Santos. In less than two weeks, he'd become an integral part of her life.

Reflections of the pool's water danced on the large screen over the bed, and the low, sweet sound of violins swept from the stereo's hidden speakers.

The hallway light sliced through the shadows to the round water bed and Nick. Propped against the elaborately padded headboard, he was bare chested, a pale satin sheet riding low on his flat tanned stomach. He rubbed a short tumbler of iced whiskey up and down his right thigh.

Closing the heavy door, Kim leaned against it, studying him. Deeply tanned, his black hair framing his face, Nick looked every particle of a lounging pirate right down to his eye patch. Yet somehow, he maintained the comforting familiarity of her well-worn terry-cloth.

He wanted her. He wanted too much. But just for tonight, she'd allow herself to feel like a woman. She needed him. Slowly, irrevocably, she turned the door lock behind her.

"Having trouble sleeping, Goldilocks?" The rough

edge of his deep voice tingled around her, luring her slowly toward his bed. Everything about Nick, she realized as he watched her approach, affected her senses. In his most vulnerable mood, Nick could wring emotions from her that she hadn't previously known. Sprawled between the light-toned sheets, surrounded by king-sized pillows, Nick looked like the singular experience of her lifetime.

It had been a long empty life. But no longer. Nick could strike her like quills of a porcupine, or he could make her want to snuggle in his arms. He made her *feel*. And she was hungry for him in a way she had never hungered before—totally, sensually—blotting out everything but his possession.

"Kim?" he asked softly, the tumbler slowing in its trail on his thigh. "What's wrong, love?"

Forcing her thoughts away from the comfort of his big body, and the strength she needed to warm her just for tonight, Kim answered truthfully, "I'm just too tired for a workout, Nick. That's how I usually come down after a hard day. But today has been—"

"I know—a real bitch." He sat the tumbler on the night stand. "Are you going to let me hold you, sweetheart? You look like you could use a friend."

"So do you, Nick." She took his hand, allowing him to draw her down into his arms.

Lying against him, her cheek resting on his chest, Kim listened to Nick's steady heartbeat. "You're a comfortable old thing."

Nick's chuckle rumbled beneath her ear. He toyed with her hair, wrapping it about his fingers. "You're the first woman to tell me that."

His right arm squeezed her lightly against his side. His breath caught and his hands stilled. "God, what have you got under that thing? You feel too soft."

"Women *are* soft, dummy." Kim giggled, rubbing his chest with her cheek. For an experienced man, Nick acted stunned. She felt her fatigue drain away, replaced by a tingling sensuality.

"I'm not up to fun and games tonight, lucky lady."
His voice was raspy, tearing the words from his throat.
His big body tensed as Kim lightly skimmed his chest
with her palm, enjoying the tickling sensation of his
hair.

"You're not going to play hard to get, are you, darling?" She flicked her tongue over his nipple and Nick
literally jumped.

"I'd like to seduce the hell out of you, Goldilocks.
But I know if you don't get out of this bed—pronto—
I'll take you any way I can get you. I don't feel very
gentle tonight." His voice was raw. He sounded like a
man at the end of a very short leash.

Kim liked that. Off-balancing this suave gambler,
this ladies' man par excellence, gave her more of a natural high than a stiff workout. She felt like the personification of ultrafemininity. *He* made her feel that way.
She trusted him. She cared for him deeply. They were
both adults with adult-sized hungers, she told herself.

Then, too, she'd always liked challenges. Pushing
her remaining reservations behind her, Kim launched a
very soft, very determined attack against Nick.

Her light kiss on his brawny padded shoulder caused
him to jackknife, sitting up. He scowled down at her.
"Look, Kim. We've both had a hard day. I've had a few
shots of whiskey, and I don't think I can control the
situation right now," he said impatiently. Taking a deep
breath in preparation for his lecture, Nick began, "A
man's bed is no place for games, Kim. Twice today,
I've nearly had you. That's enough torture for any man.
There's no backing up once we—"

"Getting old, darling? Haven't you heard? The third
try is lucky..."

He gasped as her forefinger lodged in his navel, circling it gently. The reflection of the pool water struck
the harsh planes of his face as he leaned over her, his
arms braced on either side of her head. "Do you have
any idea what you're begging for?"

"I've got a vague idea." She finger-walked over the

sheet to his thigh, caressing the strong muscles lightly. "But I'll never know, if you don't get busy."

Nick grinned slowly, sensuously. "Now that sounds like a damned hard challenge to refuse. Are you sure you know what you're doing?"

"Positive, darling. Quit talking and kiss me." Kim laced her fingers through the hair on his chest and tugged.

"Yes, sir, boss. Anything you say. . ." Nick's breath brushed her lips before his broad chest settled over hers. His eye closed slowly as he rested lightly against her. He nuzzled her throat, biting it gently as his hand smoothed her robe to find the roundness of her breast. "You've got a lot of clothes on, lucky lady."

Fascinated by the rippling muscles of his back beneath her palms and the hot, hard planes of his face pressing into her throat, Kim whispered, "Take them off, darling."

He gently eased the robe from her, throwing it to the floor. He stared down at the teddy, probing the lace to seek her nipples. Seeking them through the cloth with his open mouth, Nick blew on the damp fabric. When she gasped, he grinned. "How the devil do I get into this thing?"

Answering his own question, and in a flamboyant style all his own, Nick tore each thin strap. He slid the lace beneath her breasts and stilled, his glittering gaze devouring her flesh. "You're lovely, sweetheart," he whispered softly. "Cream and honey."

When the teddy lay discarded on her robe, Nick breathed heavily. He arranged her long curls across his pillows like an artist preparing the scene for a painting. "Beautiful," he murmured, skimming down the length of her body with his palm. "Beautiful and all mine."

Captivated by the stark hunger in his face, Kim lay still. His left hand roamed her body, exploring . . . She gasped as his fingers slid expertly between her thighs, rising slowly to the quivering core, entering her. "Nick!"

Watching her face closely, Nick murmured, "Shocked?"

Kim flushed, barely able to control the need to wrap herself around him, drawing him into her. She trembled, feeling moist and hot and hungry.

He chuckled, smoothing the jumbled curls back from her damp forehead with the fingers of his right hand. "So much passion, sweetheart. You're a very physical lady."

She writhed as he touched her. "Nick, don't play with me. I've..." Biting her bottom lip to keep from crying out, she gasped. "I'm not very experienced at this, and it's been a long time."

"That makes the taking all the sweeter, love. God, you're hot!" Taking her mouth, Nick slowly settled his chest over her breasts, tormenting her hardened nipples with the warm hair-roughened texture of his chest.

Locking her palms to his back, Kim clung to him, letting him devour her mouth almost roughly. Opening her mouth to his probing tongue, Kim strained against him as the tension within her gathered momentum, rippling through her. Then, cresting, trembling, she melted, parts of her flying off into space as his fingers plied her body. "Nick!"

Lifting his head, he smiled tenderly. "Damn. I could watch you till the earth went off its axis. You're lovely."

Lowering her lashes, Kim whispered, "It's been so long for me, Nick. I'm afraid I..." How could she say that his hands alone had taken her to the peak of lovemaking?

His teeth were white in the dimmed light. He lifted his thick eyebrows. "A man likes to know he can arouse his lady, love. It's quite a boost for the male ego. But there's more to come, sweetheart."

When Kim framed his jaw with her hands, he frowned. "Dammit. You're new to this, aren't you? You don't know how to give it back. What kind of a marriage did you have anyway?"

Ignoring the question she didn't want to answer, Kim whispered, "Teach me, Nick. Now."

Her finger traced his mouth and Nick gently bit the end of it. "For now, little one, I'll let you get by. But you've got some heavy explaining to do."

"Show me, Nick." Straining against his large body, Kim needed him desperately. She slid the sheet from his hips as she met his gaze, caressing the muscular planes of his stomach, lower...

Pressing her hand upon him intimately, Nick rolled to his back, drawing her over him. Taking her nipple in his mouth, he gently suckled until white-hot flames shot through her.

Within the valley of her breasts, Nick murmured, "God, you taste good." Raising her slightly, he bent to forage her navel with his tongue.

"Nick!" she protested as another explosion rocked her unsteady senses.

"Mmmm?" he crooned, laying back. He stroked the back of her thighs, easing her astride him.

"Nick ... what are you doing?" she managed to say, gasping as he cupped the back of her head with his hand to draw her to his hot mouth. He trailed kisses across the sensitive corners of her mouth, tantalizing her with the tip of his tongue.

"Guess," he whispered as he entered her gently.

Kim didn't know whether to bolt or fly, taking his length within her. Their journey was an explosion, a heated tangle of arms and legs and tender mouths hungrily plying each other.

Her heartbeat soared into overdrive as she met his thrusts, striving for the ultimate pleasure. "I love you, Kim," he groaned against her ear as he stilled, lifting her body tautly with his. The rippling tides washed over Kim immediately, leaving her flushed and draped over him.

Resting her face within the cove of his neck and shoulder, Kim smoothed his damp shoulders, pleasure wafting over her as his heartbeat slowed beneath her breasts.

Nick kissed her forehead, his hands stroking her back and hips. "Sweetheart, I'm going to have to start exercising more to keep up with you." He chuckled. "I've just been taken by a dynamite lady."

"Nick..." Kim liked his satisfied tone, but was embarrassed by her new-found blast of sensuality. It had taken her, thrashing against him, making her forget everything but him.

He smoothed her damp hair back from her cheek. "Shy? Sweetheart, you've just given me more pleasure than I've had in my life."

She trembled, still locked to him. Taking a deep breath, she apologized. "I'm sorry. I should have let you . . . you know."

Nick lifted her chin with his forefinger, smiling down at her gently. "Hey, who's complaining, lady?"

His kiss was tender, enveloping her in a sweet sensuality. Kim shuddered, feeling her desire rise. "But I was so aggressive, Nick."

"I know, you held nothing back, a perfect lover. I loved it, but now..." He turned her beneath him. "We can take it a little slower..."

Kim felt his pleasure as he settled within her luxuriously. He sighed, nuzzling her cheek. "Lucky lady, you're a sexy package. You purr when you make love. Your eyes turn dark and your mouth... Your mouth makes me crazy."

Enjoying the fresh intimacy with him, Kim smiled up at him, tracing the planes of his face. Trailing her lips across his, she bit him gently. "I didn't know men liked women who . . . took the lead."

"Honey, that's the biggest ego builder there is..." Nick groaned as she began to search his lean ribs with her fingers, caressing the hard mounds of his buttocks.

When his lips pressed deeply into hers, Kim gasped. "Oh, Nick! Again?"

Nick reached for her two more times in the night,

cradling her possessively to him when the morning light entered the bedroom through the window sheers.

Naked, Nick stood by the round bed in the late morning, watching Kim as she slept. It was a sight he'd remember all his life: her long hair love-tangled, her golden-tinted body barely covered by the satin sheet, one breast exposed, its pink tip enticing him.

Her face. Still flushed from their lovemaking, Kim had shadows beneath her tawny lashes. Her mouth bore a well-kissed look, and tiny swatches caused by his rough beard darkened her slender throat. Nick rubbed his jaw, the stubble grating across his palm. He'd have to shave more often—her skin was too delicate.

She sighed in her sleep, turning and running a hand over her stomach and lower, frowning slightly. She would be tender, Nick thought as she stretched sensuously. Kim hadn't been with a man for quite some time. She'd destroyed all his resolves to tantalize her sexually. He grinned. She caused a red-hot explosion when they touched—there was no holding it back.

After his shower, Nick shaved. In the steamy mirror, his face looked less drawn and he admitted the sensual ease within his body. The thought came from nowhere shattering him: Would Kim regret the past night?

She wasn't the kind of woman to enter a relationship for sexual gratification alone. She *had* to care. Didn't she?

Nick's hand shook and he nicked himself with the razor. She *had* to care . . .

Cherry tugged at the towel covering his hips. "Hi, Daddy. You cut yourself. Can I put toilet paper on it like I did last time?"

Lifting his daughter to the vanity, Nick handed her a swatch of paper. "Here, nurse. Make me well."

She concentrated on the task, her tongue sliding outside her mouth. She patted his shaven cheek, her wide blue eyes studying him. "You look different, Daddy. You're pretty when you smile."

"Pretty? Kim is pretty. I'm handsome," he teased.

Cherry giggled, then frowned. "Kimmy looked worried this morning, Daddy. She was just coming out of your bedroom when I came in. She's in her room now. She looks tired."

Nick felt a jolt of fear run through him. He'd wanted to caress her awake, to see for himself that she had no regrets. Maybe he'd pushed too hard... "We'll serve her breakfast in bed. How about that, kitten?"

His daughter's eyes lit up. "You and me make breakfast? Together?" She frowned, her finger patting the toilet paper. "Aw, you mean cereal and milk."

"Uh-uh, I'll make an omelette, little broad. You can help."

Cherry tilted her head to one side, staring at him closely. "Daddy, now that we have Kimmy, are you going to get fat and old like the other daddies?"

Tossing her in the air, Nick chuckled. "Not a chance. Kim wouldn't stand for it."

"Charles is fat," Cherry stated flatly, wrapping her arms about his neck. "I don't like him."

Later, balancing the tray before Kim's door, Nick frowned. Cherry tried the locked door, looking up at him. "She's taking a bath. I hear water running. All our fun is ruined."

His hands trembling, Nick said, "We can heat it up in the microwave later." Damn, he had to see Kim and talk to her. "Aren't cartoons on TV now? We could watch them until Kim is ready. Then we'll all go shopping for some new toys for Lassie. How about that?"

"You, Daddy? You'll take me shopping?" Cherry asked, round-eyed.

"All of us, little broad."

Nick watched a round of cartoons with his daughter, then said, "I'm going to check on Kim, Cherry."

"Bring her back here, Daddy. It's almost time for Bullwinkle," Cherry said without turning her eyes from the screen.

Letting himself into Kim's room, Nick smiled as he

listened to her humming. It was a happy sound he liked. Drawn by it, he walked toward the bathroom and his woman.

Finished with her bath, Kim wrapped the huge Turkish towel around her, tucking the edge between her breasts to form a sarong. Patting moisturizer over her face, she eased a damp strand of hair into the towel forming a turban on her head. She smiled softly at her mirrored image, feeling very tender, feeling very much like Nick's woman.

She met Nick's twinkling eye in the foggy mirror. His arms were crossed across his chest as he leaned against the bathroom door, grinning widely.

"Pleased with yourself, lucky lady?" Nick looked as sexy as his deep voice sounded, dressed in a white sweater and worn jeans that closely fitted his long muscular legs.

Kim felt the jolt of his nearness shoot down to her abdomen, lodging there, weakening her legs. Remembering their passion, she flushed, unable to look away from him.

"It was a memorable night, Nick," she whispered, wanting to move into his arms.

"Unforgettable," he agreed, reaching out to outline her breasts with his knuckles. "You were gone when I got back to bed—"

"Cherry wanted to see you and I—"

"Slipped out," he finished for her, cupping her bare shoulders with his hands. "Are you all right, Kim?"

His concern danced along her scrambled nerves. Somehow Nick managed to make her feel cherished. "I'm not quite used to those acrobatics, Nick. My muscles are a little stiff."

"Mmm," he murmured, bending to kiss her forehead. "I'll kiss them and make them well." He unwound the towel on her hair. Picking up her hair brush, he untangled her curls gently. "I've wanted to do this for a long time, honey. Come here."

Lifting her in his arms, Nick carried her to the bed.

Seated with her on his lap, he continued brushing her long hair. "You are beautiful, Kim. You make love like a dream."

"Ah, gee, shucks," Kim teased as her heart turned over. Nick's gaze worshiped her face as his large hand slid to warm her breast beneath the towel. He eased her back on the bed.

"You're uncomfortable with this, aren't you?" He gently squeezed her. "The newness of me being with you? In you?"

"Nick, don't . . . I'm not ready to talk about it."

His thick eyebrows lifted. "Oh, really? You're not closing me off, Kim. Any more than you can keep me outside a locked door."

"How did you get in anyway?" she asked, loving the smell of lime after shave and soap that clung to his skin.

"The old credit card trick." Holding her against him, Nick's left hand slid beneath the towel, rising high on her thighs. "You're sleeping with me every night, lover. Now that I've had a taste of you, I'm hungry for more."

She gasped as his broad hand fitted to her lower stomach, kneading it gently. "I'm not going to let you slip away now, Kim. You're a part of me. A part of Cherry's life, too."

Commitments. Commitments that hurt. With a dry throat, Kim searched his ebony eye. "Nick . . ."

"You can't go back, sweetheart," he stated gently. "It's too late. You cared enough to give me everything last night. There's a big difference between sex without feeling and lovemaking. I know from past experience. We made love, Kim." He smiled. "Several times, in fact."

"Such vast experience, Nick," she teased, uneasy at the hard intensity of his expression.

"You are quite an experience, lover." He sighed, leaning back against the pillows. "I'm aching this morning, too. My shrapnel isn't used to marathons."

"You should have that taken out, Nick."

He patted her bottom affectionately. "I've been thinking about it. Hell, I've got the most physical lover in town. I'd better get in shape."

Kim bit her lip, thinking about Nick's confidence. "Nick," she began slowly. "You shouldn't make too much of one night when both our defenses were down."

His expression stilled; his big body tensed next to hers. "I've wanted you from the moment I saw you, Kim. And you react to me like a volcano about to erupt. I've told you I love you. You're going to crack someday and admit the same love for me."

He was angry. She read it in the flush rising in his cheeks, in the ebony hardness of his gaze. Love. Other people had told her they loved her—in her experience the word was overused. "Nick, the situation is temporary. Once Laura—"

"Laura has nothing to do with this, Kim," he snapped, breathing hard. "It's an all-new ball game. One in which you're a definite participant. You seduced me last night. And if Cherry weren't waiting for you to watch cartoons with her, I'd make love to you until you forgot about everything else. You're mine, Kim Santos. Got it?"

"Nick, I did not seduce you!" Kim watched him stalk from the room, his limp pronounced.

"Hell. You all but poured yourself into me, woman. I call that seduction."

"Nick, you're making me angry..." she warned, feeling herself gear up for battle. He had nerve if not sensibilities. Nick was a raw-natured man. Spoiled by women, and she'd just added fuel to his enormous ego.

At the door he turned, his face grim. "Get dressed. We're taking Cherry shopping. We're going to have fun, like it or not!"

"Hey, you guys, slow down," Cherry demanded an hour later as Nick held her left hand and Kim held her right one. "I feel like a wishbone between you guys."

"We're having fun," Nick growled, leveling a dark

stare at Kim. He was careless of the other customers weaving around them in the pet store.

Kim laughed, her body vibes in tune with the frisky puppies leaping against the show window. Despite Nick's dark mood, she felt good—needed and womanly. She bent to Cherry. "He's had a hard night. He's getting old."

Nick's nostrils flared, his eyebrows locked together. Planting his hands on his lean hips, he braced his long legs apart. "Who's old?"

By the time they'd purchased Lassie's chew toys, Nick's scowl had eased. They shopped for a dress for Cherry, and she proudly modeled it at home. "I like ruffles, Kimmy. I like pink." Cherry grinned, dancing about the kitchen. "I like the pink nightgown Daddy bought for you when you weren't looking. You should go try it on for us, like I'm doing."

Nick smothered a chuckle, his mouth fighting a grin as Kim rounded on him. Eyebrows raised, he lifted his palms in a what-can-I-say gesture. He shrugged. "A replacement, my dear. I'll enjoy seeing you wear it."

She frowned at his cavalier attitude. "No gifts, Nick."

"You bought me an ice cream cone. It seemed a fair trade. You might as well know before you get on a high horse, that I've had my real-estate agent checking out likely gyms."

"Nick, don't you dare—"

"I'd dare anything, lucky lady." He caught her in his arms in an impromptu tango, much to Cherry's delight. "I'm eating sprouts and raw eggs and loving it."

She thrust her palms against his broad chest. His humor was infectious, his grin disarming. She'd have to watch him now; he absolutely oozed male confidence. And he possessed the neat trick of sliding under her defenses.

Nick's busy fingers tickled her and Kim arched against him, giggling. "Stop, Nick. I can't stand it."

He swooped, tossed her in the air, just as Cherry

clapped her hands. "More, Daddy. More. Make Kimmy laugh."

Nick laughed, lightly throwing Kim to the couch and stripping her heels from her. "Help me, little broad. I bet her feet are ticklish."

Laughing until her sides ached, Kim reached for him, racing her fingers across his lean ribs. "You'll pay for this, mister," she warned, giggling. Off-balance, laughing, Nick rolled to the sunlit carpet on the floor and Cherry sat on his chest. Lassie licked his face as Kim tickled him.

"Hey! Three against one isn't fair," Nick protested, catching Kim to him.

Smiling, feeling a part of his life, Kim met his twinkling stare. "Hello, honey," he said softly, stroking her cheek with his fingertips. "Welcome home."

The bottom dropped out of Kim's defenses, her heart filling at the tenderness in his expression. If she weren't careful, Nick Santos would have her lock, stock, and barrel, just as he'd promised.

"Are you going to seduce me again tonight, honey?" he asked when Cherry had skipped from the room.

"I've never seduced anyone in my entire life, Nick," she protested, laughing. "You've got your women mixed up."

"Uh-uh. There's only one of you, sweetheart," he murmured, drawing her mouth to his. "There's only one classy, hot-blooded lover."

She trailed her fingertips across his jaw. Nick was exciting, responding to her touch as his gaze darkened sensuously. "I've got whisker burn in the most unlikely places, Nick."

"I'm sorry about that, Kim. I promise I'll be more careful," he whispered, watching her. "This . . . sharing is new to you, isn't it? He had to dominate you in bed, didn't he, Kim? Small men, feeling threatened, often do that."

Quietly, she traced his prominent cheekbones, lacing

her fingers in his hair. He was right, of course. "Do we have to talk about it, Nick? I'd rather forget."

Cradling her cheek with his warm palm, he kissed her tenderly. "It's a new life, honey, for both of us. Give in to it."

CHAPTER TEN

FOUR DAYS LATER, during an afternoon shopping trip to the corner market, Cherry settled into a grocery cart seat and said, "Daddy is happy, Kimmy. He laughs a lot since you're here. I think he likes to tease you, 'cause you turn red and get all hot-looking," she announced, munching on a cookie and wiping her fingers on the teddy bear pattern of her play dress. "Especially when he chases you into a corner and kisses you . . . my watch said he kissed you for five minutes one time." She frowned. "How do you breathe when you kiss? Let's get Lassie some doggie cookies, too," she added, pointing to the dog food.

Dressed in red shorts and a red and navy striped T-shirt, Kim had to get out of the house, away from Nick's happy anticipation. Humming, "Tonight, to-night . . ." he had her nerves vibrating. And putting off Nick hadn't been easy since their night of lovemaking. "Your daddy is going to get paid back one day, Cherry. I've been thinking of tying him in a sheet and tickling him until he promises not to tease me anymore."

"Can I help? I've got good tickling fingers," the little girl asked.

"You betcha. We'll catch him before he wakes up in the morning," Kim promised.

Exiting the small market, holding Cherry's hand and

balancing a sack of groceries with her other arm, Kim walked straight into Laura, looking furious, her eyes skimming over them with all the friendliness of a hungry barracuda. A gust of wind lashed sand against their ankles, and Laura grimaced. "How I hate this eternal sand—the weather here is terrible on my complexion . . . I've talked to a lawyer. He says I can take Cherry any time I want. And I want her now. You can't stop me."

Cherry's chubby face began to pucker, her eyes teary as she wrapped her arms around Kim's bare leg. "Kimmy?"

Kim rested her free hand on Cherry's hunched shoulder. She doubted that Laura's lawyer had made the statement. "Laura, you're not taking Cherry without a court decree," Kim stated more coolly than she felt. What type of mother would frighten her own child?

"Oh, I've got legal papers. A judge signed them this morning. She's mine now; it's in black and white," Laura hissed. "Come along now, Cherry. Charles is waiting."

"Kimmy?!" Cherry's distressed cry shot up between them.

"We're going home now," Kim said tightly, positive that Laura was lying through her teeth. "Call Nick to discuss your problems tonight. I'll tell him I talked to you."

"*I* don't have to wait. I'm her mother, and I'm taking her now!" Laura shrieked, reaching for Cherry.

She needed a lesson in manners, Kim thought, stepping between Cherry and her mother. Sobbing frantically, Cherry clutched Kim's bare leg with all her might.

"Stop that sniveling, Cherry. Now!" Laura screamed, trembling beneath her raw silk jacket. "See what you've done, you . . . bimbo? You're scaring the hell out of her!"

"Bimbo?" Kim questioned quietly before she sat the groceries on the sidewalk. "Did you say bimbo?"

"Give her to me. I have to have her!" Laura screamed, trying to get past Kim to Cherry.

Fighting to remain cool, Kim took a deep breath. She placed the flat of her hand on Laura's chest to thrust her backward. "Call Nick later, Laura. He'll be expecting your call," she repeated. "But for now, you're not taking Cherry."

Scathingly, Laura's eyes ran down the golden length of Kim's legs. "Look at you. What he sees in you, I don't know. You've positively got muscles bulging everywhere."

"I like to stay in shape. And I'd really like to give you a lesson in manners, Laura, if you frighten Cherry anymore," Kim said quietly.

"Oh, I just bet you would. I understand you're a female jock. You and Nick suit each other—you're both too . . . primitive for words!" Laura snapped. "I'll let her go for now, but I'll be back."

Seated on her father's lap after dinner, Cherry frowned. "She's a mean woman, Daddy. But she was scared of Kimmy. Kimmy said she wanted to teach her manners. I'd lay forty-to-one odds on Kimmy, Daddy."

Grim-faced, Nick stroked Cherry's tousled hair. Meeting Kim's eyes as she paced the living room, he said, "I'll make sure this doesn't happen again. My attorney says we can get an injunction, legally keeping Laura away from Cherry."

"See that you do, Nick," Kim agreed. "She says she has a judge's signature for custody, but I doubt it. The woman is dying to get her hands on Cherry."

"She's bluffing. I'll take care of it tonight, Kim. Relax, will you? You look like you're ready to explode, fireball," Nick said gently. "It fascinates the hell out of me when you bounce around like a ball in a pinball machine, ready to pounce. You're charged up enough to run ten miles tonight, Kim."

"You should know how I feel. Laura's not exactly a model mother." She did a double take, examining

Nick's slow, wide grin. It read as plainly as Las Vegas neon lights, filled with sensual anticipation.

"Lassie needs his doggie cookies. We're going outside to my new gym set. I'll swing him." Cherry slipped from his lap, calling the frolicking puppy.

Nick leaned back against the couch. "I'll take care of Laura. She won't bother Cherry again," he said before the timbre of his voice lowered. "Come here, sweetheart. Take it all out on me," he whispered, blowing her a kiss. "Use me . . . I don't care."

Growing hot and trembling as he stared at her, she protested, "Nick! Your mother and Cherry are in the house . . . How can you think of a thing like that now?"

"You need an attitude adjustment, woman. I said I'd take care of it, and I will—you need to trust me. And kiss me. If you don't come here, I'll come get you," Nick threatened, grinning as he rose slowly from the couch.

"Nick, you wouldn't dare—" Kim began as he stalked toward her. "Nick?"

"'Methinks the lady doth protest too much,'" he quoted, reaching for her as she danced out of the way. "Come here, you hot little tamale."

Kim giggled, feeling giddy as Nick practiced his leer. "All you need is a gold tooth, and you'd make a perfect pirate."

"Pirates have love slaves tied to the bedposts, m'love. I'm ready if you are," he tossed back, grinning. "Speaking of beds, you're sharing mine tonight, aren't you?"

Remembering his tender passion, Kim trembled, her eyes locked to the darkness of his gaze. "Nick, one night of—"

"A momentary weakness, is that how you think of it, Kim?" he asked softly, thrusting his fingers through her hair to bring her face to his. His right hand pressed her hips against his. "It's a fire raging in my blood, sweetheart." He searched her face. "And it's more—it's love, like it or not." Stroking the roundness of her hip, he kissed her lightly. "You were almost virginal. Did I hurt you?"

"I did ache, Nick," she whispered, feeling her body melting, responding to his warmth. "I haven't had the practice you have."

"Mmmm. Different muscles than aerobics, huh? Practice makes perfect, my love. Move into my bed to stay," Nick coaxed before his mouth covered her parted lips. Drawing her into his arms, Nick trailed kisses across her hot face. When his head lifted, Kim swayed toward him, her arms locked about his neck. He grinned wryly. "Funny. I thought I was too old to hear bells when I kissed my girl."

Pressing her face against his shoulder, Kim looked at him through her lashes. She enjoyed his lighthearted mood—enjoyed throwing it back at him. "You're probably gearing up for a heart attack."

"What a way to go, lucky lady." He laughed.

"Temper, temper," Duke teased as he spread his royal flush on the casino's table two nights later. Seated near Kim, he sprawled across the small chair.

Kim frowned down at her two pair of kings, thumping her fingers on the green felt. Nick resembled the king of spades, she thought darkly, comparing the card's split images with Nick's changing personality. In the three weeks she had known him, he could tease her until she giggled, or he could storm until she wanted to tangle outright with him. Either way, by their lovemaking last week, he had clearly devastated her resolve to remain in control of the situation.

"Come on, honey chil'. It's a slow night. I'm waiting for my buyer to make up his mind about some property in Las Vegas and you're not all that busy. Give . . . what's the problem? You're actually pouting, pretty girl. Tell old dad all about it." Duke grinned. "I'm all ears."

"You wouldn't understand, Duke." Kim barely understood the situation herself. Tonight Nick had a big

DANGER sign pasted all over his lean body; his dazzling smile alone could disarm a Doberman pinscher.

A delivery boy tapped Kim's bare shoulder. His arms were loaded with three-dozen red roses, their long stems wrapped in green tissue paper. "Mrs. Santos?" When Kim nodded, the boy handed the roses to her. "Sign for receipt please, ma'am."

She shot a frown at Duke's snicker. "Don't say anything cute, Duke," she warned tightly.

"Why, honey chil', I was just thinking how nice those roses match your yellow silk dress," he remarked mildly, fighting his grin. "Aren't you going to read the card?" He glanced at the bold scrawl. "Huh. I wonder what this means—it says 'Tonight.'"

"Duke! Mind your own business," Kim reprimanded.

"They're from Mr. Santos, sir," the delivery boy said, walking toward the door. "Thank you for the signature, ma'am."

"Wow. Old Nick's got him a live one, I'd say," Duke teased. "You're blushing, sweetie. Can't you take the heat?"

Kim stared at him, frowning as she remembered the ruffly pink nightgown arranged on her bedspread. Attached was a scrawling note, "Replacement." She felt rushed and hot and disheveled every time he leveled that singular black eye at her. She wasn't in the mood for teasing. "Shut up, Duke."

Duke's grin died. "I'm a good listener, Kim. Don't tell me you don't need one. You look like you're going to explode. Even Laura couldn't have ruffled your feathers that much. Nick's right in there pitching and you're balking, right?"

"Something like that, Duke. The man has probably never experienced a 'no' in his entire lifetime." Off-balance, Kim had to clutch something real. She chose Duke's big hand.

His fingers locked with hers and his arm circled her bare shoulders. He squeezed her in a comforting gesture. "I said I'd be around for you, honey. But I'm beginning to think three is a crowd in this romance. I don't think these Texan bones can take the fire between you two."

"Stop handling the merchandise, Duke," Nick warned behind them. "I never thought I'd catch you trying to make time with *my wife*."

Kim stood shakily, wondering if the teasing man of the afternoon had been a mirage, replaced by the reality of Nick's angry face—the flip side of the king of spades, she thought.

Duke rose to meet Nick's fierce expression. "No one is cheating on you, Nick—"

She bumped Duke's chest with her shoulder. "Don't you dare apologize, Duke. My master allows me friends."

"*Women* friends, Kim—" Nick began hotly, interrupted by Kim slashing the huge bouquet of roses across his black tuxedo.

He wiped a red petal from his bottom lip and glared at her.

"He does *not* sleep with every woman he meets, Nick. I asked him," she stated tightly. Enraged, Nick looked as if he'd like to start a brawl. Well, not if she started one first.

"You asked him *that?*" Nick blazed, his fists tightening.

"Now, buddy—" Duke began carefully before Kim and Nick both stared at him. "I feel like a skunk strolling down the deodorant section in a supermarket," he mumbled.

"Butt out," the Santoses warned in unison.

"Whoa!" Duke's green eyes widened. "If you two are going to deck me, I'd like to know why."

Nick glowered at him. "If I were you, I'd pack it on back to Texas."

Kim grabbed the strings of Duke's turquoise western necktie, staying him by her side. She thumped Nick's chest with the huge bouquet and red petals flew up into his black hair, fluttering down on his black tuxedo and shoulders. "He's my friend and he's staying."

"Like hell," Nick shouted. "You've been giving my lady driving lessons, Duke. As of now they're canceled. She'll drive my Porsche, like it or not!"

Kim tugged on Duke's tie and thumped Nick again with the roses. She was furious at Nick, but after all, Duke was his friend and he deserved a little taking down, too. The two of them had probably womanized across the entire Silver State and back again.

"I'll play you for her, Duke," Nick growled, his jaw jutting over Kim's head.

"Hey, buddy—" Duke protested as Kim shoved him backward, turning fully to Nick.

"What . . . did . . . you . . . say, Nick?" she asked softly. Every corpuscle in her taut body wanted to launch into Nick. Did he think he had owner's papers?

He slashed a glance down at her, the muscles in his jaw flexing as if his teeth ground against each other. "A winner-take-all game. His oil wells against my casino and property holdings—condos *and* mines. It's an even bet, Kim."

"You said you'd play for *me*, Nick. *I'm* not property." Kim wanted to shred the bouquet and make him eat it.

"You're *my* wife!" Nick roared.

"Ooooo," Kim groaned, trembling and momentarily speechless. "Oooo . . . then *I'll* play you."

Duke glanced around at the gathering crowd. "Hey, you guys. Watch it, you're creating a scene."

Kim thrust the bouquet at him. "Here. Make yourself useful; hold this." She stalked toward the casino office, turned, and glared at Nick. "Coming, dear?"

"Damn right, I am, *dear*."

Locking the door behind him, Nick watched Kim stalk across the red carpet, her yellow silk dress swirling, clinging to the lines of her body. In a rage, Kim had to be the most beautiful woman in the world, he thought. The sexiest. The most irritating, stimulating woman of his lifetime.

She rounded on him, her hands on her waist and her shapely legs taut against the constriction of the knee-length dress. A slit exposed the curve of her left thigh.

Her hand slashed the air, her hair tangling about her shoulders as she faced him. "Bought and paid for. Is *that* your attitude, mister? All my friends have to pass the Santos clearance test? You had no right to throw a winner-takes-all game at him."

"You look like a fireball, lady. You give off any more energy and you'll start a fire," he growled, feeling off-stride. He'd planned a night of romance—but he'd exploded when he saw Duke holding Kim. But he didn't intend to back up now. Like it or not, *he* was the only man in her life.

"Okay, gambler man. We're playing for me, aren't we? *You* consider me a piece of property, with no options. *I* have options running out of my ears and I'm feeling lucky. Name the game—I'm ready to play," Kim demanded.

"There are a lot of games I want to play with you, honey," Nick said evenly. His palms tingled as he remembered the silkiness of her skin.

"Great. What are the stakes?" she shot back at him.

Nick's heart thudded heavily against his ribs. The week since they'd made love had been the longest in his life. He wanted her naked—in his arms. "Five-card draw—strip poker."

She crossed her arms over her chest, one silk-clad toe tapping the red carpet. "Only you would think of something like that. Well, you can't win all the time. If I win, I'm taking your clothes and walking out of here."

Her blue eyes ran over him. "I'm wearing two diamond earrings, a dress, briefs, and two shoes." She leaned back against the desk and stared at him. "How many clothes are you wearing?"

He kicked off his shoes, tearing off his jacket and discarding his tie. "A shirt, belt, two socks, slacks, and shorts. I'll spot you since you're not in my league." He tugged off his belt and socks.

"And we'll count those strings supporting your dress," he offered, touching the small straps before she could step back. "I need the experience of tearing clothes off you, like *that* night." Nick's throat went dry as Kim took a deep steadying breath. The shimmering fullness of her breasts rose above the yellow bodice.

"Mister, you have a bet. Las Vegas doesn't experience a Lord Godiva every day. At least not walking through the casino." Kim stalked toward the table, sitting stiffly in a chair.

Later, minus her earrings and her shoes, Kim mentally chastised herself. Why did she seem to lose control when Nick Santos was near her? Now he stared at her. "Nervous, pretty lady? You lost before. Why did you want to play a second time?" he asked.

She answered honestly. "Because you make me so mad. The game's not over."

"Damn right, it's not. I'm a little tense myself. Deal." He shoved the deck toward her and grinned.

Kim shuffled the cards expertly, feeling his gaze heat her flesh, riveting on her low-cut bodice. "Do you have to be so . . . primitive?"

Nick's eyebrows lifted. "You could domesticate the holy hell out of me, lady. And you know it."

She dealt and lost the hand. Nick leaned back in his chair, crossed his arms, then asked, "Now what? You don't have on nylons, so that leaves the dress and your panties."

Kim was angry. "You said you'd spot me the straps."

"So I did." Before she could move, he reached toward her, snapping free one of her straps.

"Oh!" Kim tugged up the sagging corner of her bodice. "You didn't have to ruin the dress."

"I'm not in a pleasant mood, lady," he growled. "I had other plans for the evening . . . a midnight dinner and champagne for two in the suite upstairs. Where you can make all the sweet little noises you want."

He glanced at her sagging bodice as he dealt the cards. "Are you going to fight me all the way, lover? Cards?"

Kim quickly wound the joined straps around her neck and tied the broken end to the good strap. She didn't like his smile as she tugged her bodice upward, then quickly arranged her cards in her hand.

Kim lost the hand and braced herself when he reached toward her. He tore the second strap from its mooring. "I'll get you another dress—one with straps." He trailed a long dark finger across her collarbone and straight down into the crevice between her breasts. His hand slid across her breast then up to cup her shoulder briefly. Kim trembled, feeling her body heat at his touch.

He glanced at her fingers gripping her bodice. One black eyebrow raised. "You have lovely breasts, Kim," he said huskily. "Sweet-scented and filling my hands. They taste—"

"How dare you talk about that now!" If Kim could have freed her hands, she would have adjusted his taunting attitude.

"I've got a hunger for you, lady. And I need you hungry for me . . . needing me, with those tender little groans driving me crazy." He dealt the last card. "What's next? The dress or your panties?"

"As I understand the rules, it's my choice," she snapped. "You might as well deal—my hands are busy." Nick laid her passions out before her like his cards. Did the man know anything about a lady's sensibilities?

He shuffled and dealt the cards with a dexterity faster than Superman's speeding bullet, she thought. Warily, she studied her hand. "Cards?" he asked, gazing at her lips.

"Yes, thank you!" Kim discarded four cards and Nick dealt their replacements. He replaced two of his cards and lifted his brow.

"Well?" he asked as he laid down his cards. Kim

blinked, wishing his joker and four aces—a top poker hand, called five of a kind—would somehow disappear. Those cards beat her royal flush.

"I'd appreciate it if you'd discard the dress first," Nick drawled.

Without thinking, Kim glared at him, stood, supported her dress with one hand, and edged her other hand beneath her dress. He couldn't have his way all the time, she promised. She tugged, wriggling out of her briefs. She tossed the string and lace garment onto the table. "Damn you, Nick."

He probed the delicate thong briefs with the tip of his finger, hooked one of the hip strings, and dangled it before him. "Interesting."

Kim plopped into her chair, rigid with anger. "I'm sure you've seen that kind before. Probably *many* times before."

The nude-colored lace swayed before him like a trophy. Nick examined it thoroughly, holding it up to the light. "Not exactly. Bikinis, yes. But underwear fashioned like a G-string, no. What's the advantage?"

She did not intend to discuss the intricacies of her underclothing with him, Kim decided. He kept examining the panties and finally straightened them on the table. "Well?"

"The strings are fitted to the waist, leaving no panty line at the hips. A dress like this demands a minimum of underclothing," Kim almost yelled. She had lost control of her clothing, her nerves, and her life. She might as well go for broke.

Kim braced her left arm on the table, nestled her breasts over it, and tried as best she could to support her bodice with her fingers. "Are you going to deal the last hand or not?"

"Naturally." His hands moved smoothly, quickly dealing the cards. When she'd lost one last time, Kim decided to end the charade.

She stood, turned, and searched for the zipper behind her back. It slid open smoothly, and Nick's warm hands swept over her back, cupped her shoulders, and turned her around as the dress slithered to the floor.

He breathed deeply, his gaze traveling down, then up, her body. "Now that's more like it."

Placing his hands alongside her cheeks, he drew her lips to his. "You rise to the bait so beautifully, lover. I can't help myself. I'm sorry. I'm sorry about jumping Duke, too. I'll even apologize to him."

Tenderly tracing the pad of his thumb across her bottom lip, Nick grinned wryly. "Smile. You know you want to."

Tugging at her vulnerable side, Nick was more devastating than when he was angry, she decided. He made her feel wobbly and warm every time he touched her. In fact—the thought hit her with deadly impact—she loved him, his tenderness, his responsiveness to her lonely background, his gentleness. But if she admitted that love to Nick now, he'd take it and run like a football player on an empty field. She couldn't handle that —not yet.

Placing her fingers on his wrists, she asked, "What have I got to smile about? You're the one with clothes."

"I'll take them off if you want—" he offered.

"Nick!"

Trailing his tongue across her upper lip, Nick groaned. "I love you, lucky lady. When are you going to stop fighting me?"

"I can't. You're too deadly. You want too much . . ." Kim said huskily as her knees went weak and her hands found his waist as if magnetized.

His eye skimmed her face and he smiled gently. "You gave yourself to me that night we found Cherry, lover. A total commitment you've never given any man before. The earth went off its axis. Again and again. That's got to count for something."

Kim lowered her lids, not wanting him to see into the heart of her.

He kissed her closed lids. "If you'd admit you cared about me, you wouldn't be wound so tight, sweetheart."

He shook her head gently. "Admit it. I'm the only man in your life."

Feeling her way, Kim said, "I am fond of you."

"Fond? Now that's a hell of a word. I'm in love with you, lady. Nonstop . . . all the way," Nick stated huskily. His kiss was tender and searching and hungry. "You're not immune to me, Kim. Why are you fighting me and what we could have?"

"You push too much, Nick. I'm not made to be pushed," Kim said against his mouth.

"Learn. We can make this marriage work, sweetheart." Sweeping her against him, Nick's large hands swept down to her hips. He cupped her softness, lifting her against him as his kiss seared her mouth.

CHAPTER ELEVEN

"LAURA HAS LEFT town on her broom," Nick said, watching Kim do her cool-down exercises the next morning. "My lawyer checked this morning."

The bright sun filtered into the room from the skylight, gilding the mass of long curls and the perfect curves of her body beneath the pink leotard and matching leg warmers. Straightening, her left leg extended and the right one bent beside her, Kim looked at him, her expression unreadable. A pale, strained look underlined the flush caused by the energetic dance routines. Her fingers trembled as they circled her bare foot in a leg stretch. "I'm glad. She terrified Cherry."

"You've been working out all morning, Kim." There was something in her expression, in the tension of her body that worried him. The wager was complete now—would Kim leave him? "Cherry and Mom are worried about you."

Touching her forehead to her left knee, Kim said, "I'm just doing my usual workout."

Nick rubbed the back of his neck. The taut cords complemented his throbbing headache. "Kim, believe it or not, I didn't mean to come on to you like gangbusters last night. I meant to . . . romance you. Well, it didn't go the way I'd planned."

She looked at him steadily. "It wasn't anyone's fault

that we ended up making love on the floor, Nick. It just happened."

He rubbed his palm across his jaw, feeling suddenly old and tired. "Damn. You looked so shattered, Kim. But I didn't force you. I'm sorry."

"You catch me off guard, Nick. And you push. I'm thirty-five, and do you know I've never . . . never made love on the floor?"

"Hell, I said I'm sorry—" he began, impatient with the stiffness between them. "For the place. Not for the action." Instinctively, he stepped into each opportunity to push her, and he had frightened her. But it was so hard when he loved every contrary, delectable inch of her.

"I've made a decision about us, Kim," he began, feeling his stomach knot as she looked up at him.

"Oh?" The cool tone shot icily through him. Kim was placing him at a distance, her reserve restored. Maybe he *had* pushed too hard, too soon . . .

Nick took the biggest wager of his life, laying all his cards on the table. "Now you're under no obligation to us—Cherry and me. You can run all you want, little girl, and that still won't keep me from loving you. I'll be here when you need me. I'll keep my part of the bargain, a check and no strings." The promise tore into him. He wanted to say: Stay and be my love, lady. Hell, it didn't even matter if she loved him or not. He'd take whatever he could get.

Kim stared up at him evenly. "Is this reverse psychology?"

"I don't have a degree in psychology, sweetheart. But loving you, I feel alive, really alive. And I don't really know how to handle you. You're too . . . volatile."

Her eyes widened. "Me, volatile? You were ready to fight your best friend."

"I . . . ah, get a little edgy—" Why did she make him feel like a repentant schoolboy? "Okay, I get jealous. I'm made that way. But I'm not too sure where I stand with you."

Surprising him, Kim shook her head. "I'm not too sure about that myself." Rubbing her face with a towel, she gracefully rose to stand next to him. Tilting her head to one side, Kim traced the darkness beneath his eye, her finger trailing down his cheek. "I think you could be my friend," she said slowly and thoughtfully.

Nick's heart went thudding out of control, his body locked by the tenseness of his muscles. He wanted to sweep her to him, love the daylights out of her, but he wouldn't. He wouldn't until she came to him. He swallowed, watching her study him intently. What was she thinking?

"I love you, lady," he said. "I've had this feeling that you might be thinking about leaving me. Are you?"

"As a matter of fact, I have thought about it," she said firmly. "I can't think clearly around you."

Think? He still had a chance. He had to say, "It's not only sex, Kim. Remember that."

Kim's blue eyes followed her fingertip as it traced his lips. She smiled softly. "We fight, Nick. Like cats and dogs. A little old for that, aren't we?"

When her touch trailed down his throat, Nick went stock still. Damn, he wanted to hold her. But he wouldn't pressure her. Not now. They were too close . . .

Unbuttoning the first two buttons of his cotton shirt, Kim flattened her hand over his powerful muscles, tracing the planes slowly. "You're a sexy man, Nick Santos. Passionate and potent enough to shake a woman's resolve not to love again."

He breathed lightly, letting her touch stalk his body. It was not one of the easier things to do in his worldly life. Her husky voice was low, coming slowly, thoughtfully, across her soft lips. Nick knew she weighed her emotions truthfully now. When her hand lowered to his navel, following the trail of hair, he trembled, his body hardening.

She smiled up into his face, and it was a soft, tender smile, acknowledging his reaction to her touch. "I love your daughter, Nick. And I've never felt more accepted at any time in my life."

Nick cleared his throat, feeling a suspicious dampness behind his lid. She may not out and out love him, but damn, he had a chance... "Where is all this leading, honey?"

"There are old ghosts, Nick. I keep feeling that everything is too good to be true. That somehow, some way, it's all going to get jerked from me," she whispered.

Her helpless expression tore at him. "Not a chance, honey. Trust me."

"That's the strange thing. I do trust you. You're possessive and arrogant. An opportunist down to your bones. But I do trust you, Nick. I really need to work this out myself." Stepping back from him, she frowned. "I have to place everything in perspective, Nick. It's my way."

"I know," he said, wondering if he really did understand.

She grinned up at him, and he blinked, dazzled by her warmth. "I doubt it, Nick. You're perfectly willing to let your instincts rule you. It's one of your more endearing traits."

Now Nick's instincts told him to let Kim call the shots. "When you get everything down pat, will you let me know?"

"Right after the surgery, Nick. I want you to have that operation."

He looked into her blue eyes and felt himself drowning in them. "Will you hold my hand, lucky lady?"

She smoothed back the silver hair at his temples. "I'll be right there, gambler man."

A week and a half later, Nick had arranged his businesses to allow him recovery time. His surgery was performed in the early May morning.

"He's going to the recovery room now, Mrs. Santos. We'll watch him for a while before taking him back to his room. He fought the anesthetic, but the operation was a success. I saved that piece of shrapnel. You might want to make a paperweight out of it. Dastardly little piece of iron lodged in the *rectus femoris* muscle of his thigh. Rubbing around in there, it caused a lot of scar tissue that we had to work around," the doctor said, taking off his blue operating cap. "He'll be up and dancing in about three weeks. I'll give you a list of therapy exercises. He'll have to start those as soon as we remove the outer stitches. I'll check in with you later."

Kim stared down at Nick, stretched out between the sheets of the hospital cart. A tube dripped glucose into the needle in his arm. His black eyelashes and eyebrows slashed across his rugged, pale face and she had to touch him.

The doctor's hand on her arm startled her. "Are you feeling all right, Mrs. Santos? You look very white."

"I'll be fine. Thank you," she managed to say. "I . . . it's a shock to see him like this . . . he's so vital."

"Well, he will be again. You can follow the nurse into recovery if you wish," the doctor offered.

"I'll call his mother first. She needs to know the operation was a success." Kim called Maria, then found the recovery room.

Nick's condition, deathly quiet now, frightened her. As the nurse took his vital signs, Kim asked, "May I hold his hand? I'd like him to know I'm here."

"Surely. He's a handsome man, Mrs. Santos." The nurse smiled. "You must be Kim. He told me he loved me as he was going under the anesthetic. He thought he held your hand. Goodness, he could certainly turn a girl's head if he wanted to, but then I suppose you know that. He was very worried what you would think when you saw him without his eye patch . . . we'll replace it before he fully recovers. Let me know if you need anything, dear."

The hours stretched by in the hospital's hushed silence as Kim held Nick's large hand. Tracing the back of it with her thumb, from the hair-roughened texture to the large knuckles, Kim's heart contracted as his fingers locked with hers. His mouth, already shadowed by dark stubble, formed her name silently.

Suddenly, her face was damp, tears flowing onto the hospital sheet that covered his stomach. She loved him. Every arrogant, possessive bone. Every sweet, tender gesture. It was so simple. He was hers . . . she was his. For eternity. And she had loved him before their night of passion, she realized now.

She had to tell him of her love. Bending over him, Kim kissed his lips, and felt them stir against hers. "I love you, darling. I love you."

His lashes fluttered, his mouth forming her name.

"Sleep, darling. I'll be here, loving you, when you wake up," Kim whispered, kissing his cheek.

Dozing in the hospital chair in Nick's private room, Kim heard his dry whisper. "Kim—"

Rising and feeling the long fifteen hours in the confinement of the hospital, she stretched, straightening her rose-colored sweater and slacks.

Nick's eye was open, the long fringe of lashes shadowing his high cheekbone as dawn came through the window. His tongue dampened his lips and Kim smiled. "Thirsty, darling?"

She spooned chips of ice into his mouth and he sucked them, watching her intently. Setting the glass aside, Kim looked down at him tenderly, smoothing his curls from his temples. "The man I love," she whispered. Nick was asleep before she kissed him. His mouth had the slightest curl to it and she traced it slowly, enjoying the silence to study him.

Just before the nurse brought Kim's noon dinner tray, Nick groaned, his head turning on the pillow. Instantly, she was by his side. "Are you in pain, Nick?"

"Kiss me . . . and tell me you love me again . . ." he demanded unsteadily. Humoring him, Kim placed her lips on his. "I love you, darling."

"Good. I deserve it," he murmured, a touch of his arrogance returning as he drifted off into sleep.

Later that afternoon, Maria, Duke, Cherry, and Kim talked softly as Nick dozed. "He's quite manageable lying that way," Kim teased, stroking the thick line of his eyebrows.

"Huh, don't count on it lasting," Duke warned, stretching his boots before him and eyeing a pretty nurse passing in the hallway. "I heard from the military medics that sedated or not, he could raise holy hell."

"My daddy is nice, Uncle Duke," Cherry stated hotly. "He's especially nice since Kim lives with us."

"She's done some taming. I'm certain of that," Maria added.

"What? Who's done some taming?" Nick asked faintly, stirring on the bed.

"Me, you great big hunk." Kim laughed. Even in his woozy state, Nick's male antennae were alert. "You're putty in my hands," she teased.

"Huh," he stated skeptically. "You wouldn't be so cocky if I were in fighting shape." Opening his eye, he ordered, "Tilt this thing up, will you, Kim? There's a thing to turn at the end of the bed."

"Yes, sir, boss," Kim teased.

Nick grimaced. "You'd better watch out, lady. I'll remember all this when I get out of here."

"That gives me a week of teasing you, mean old thing," Kim said softly, feeling breathless as Nick's gaze stroked her face and down her body.

"I'll show you *old*, woman . . ." he threatened with a smile that stopped Kim's heart. A dazzling, blockbuster of male sensuality on the prowl.

Duke sighed. "They're at it again. Hey, buddy. Before you two lock horns, I want to give you my wedding gift . . . my half of our cabin at Lake Mead. You might want to slip away there to . . . ah . . ." His voice drifted off as his blush rose.

Nick chuckled. "I get the picture. Thanks, Duke."

Duke took a deep breath, looking from Kim to Nick. "You never had anything to worry about, Nick. You know that, don't you?"

Cherry peeked beneath the sheet covering Nick's bandaged leg. "Oh, he worries about stuff, Uncle Duke. Like when Lassie wets on his expensive shoes or chews the paper."

Nick sighed deeply, shaking his head as he reached for Kim's hand. "Mom, I love you all, but do you suppose . . . ?"

Maria laughed, lifting Cherry to kiss him. "Say good-bye to your daddy, honey. Come along, Duke. I think they want some privacy. We'll come back in the evening visiting hours, Nick."

Nick's eyebrows lifted meaningfully at Kim. "*You* stay, woman."

After they'd gone, he tugged her hand and ordered quietly, "Come here."

His look at her was dark and smoldering; Kim's body started tingling. She leaned across him, rubbing his nose with hers. "You called, master?"

"Tell me you love me again, Kim."

Not willing to obey him easily, Kim wove finger trails through his thick hair. "Maybe. Maybe not."

"Woman . . ." he growled, grinning. His hand caught her hair, easing her face to his. "Tell me."

"Tell you what? That you need a shave? I'll be glad to shave you, Nick," she teased, loving the new give-and-take between them.

"Grrrr. Lady, quit torturing me." His fingers stroked her face lightly. He smiled tenderly. "Okay. You can tell me in your own way. In your own time. In the mean-time . . ."

His kiss told her of his desire. His trembling, reverent touch told her of his love.

One week later, Nick returned home.

Kim sensed a tenseness between them in the next week as he recovered. Nick's kisses were tempered and controlled. It was as if he were waiting . . .

"Mom and Cherry have taken Lassie to the veterinarian. How about taking me for a drive? I could use the fresh air," Nick suggested Tuesday morning as he lounged in the sun and Kim swam lengths in the pool.

She shook water from her face, lifting herself from the pool easily. She patted the towel across her, accepting the lazy way his large hand circled her ankle. His thumb caressed her skin. She smiled down at him. "You've got that look, Nicholas A. Santos. What are you up to?"

He shrugged. "I feel like a prisoner, lady. I'm so desperate, I'll even let you drive your monster."

Kim laughed. "Uh-huh. You can't fold into your Porsche now. But I will take you for a drive."

"In a few minutes, honey?" he pressed.

Later, following Nick's directions, Kim parked in front of a downtown building. Paper stretched across the windows concealing the interior. Nick opened his door, easing out to stand on the sidewalk. "I've got the key to this place. Want to look around, Kim?"

The interior of the brick building was alive with workmen. Nick placed his hand on the flat of Kim's back and urged her past carpenters laying a wooden floor. "Let's step into the office," he said, opening a door.

Kim felt his tension and saw the lines on his face deepen with concern. Nick was wary. "What is this building, Nick?" she asked quietly, looking around the expensively decorated office.

For an answer, he drew away a large cloth covering a billboard that leaned against a wall. The sign read: "Kim's Gym—aerobics, self-defense, saunas."

Slowly realizing that he had purchased the building for her, Kim lifted her gaze to Nick's uncertain one. He looked like a small boy caught at the candy jar. It was an endearing expression.

Yet a twinge of anger circled Kim. Nick just had to waltz into her business, her life. She had managed her life to suit her until now.

"Am I in trouble, honey?" he probed tentatively, watching her face. His fingers trembled as he pushed them through his hair. He frowned, his expression hardening. Nick was nervous and frightened, his face darkening as if he realized he'd blundered. "Why don't you say something? Look. It's a gift. Free and clear."

Kim felt the warmth begin inside her, the glowing, loving warmth. Fletch was right. Nick was a softy. A possessive, arrogant, tender softy who looked like he'd be crushed if she didn't accept his gift. Perhaps it was time to change her life and allow Nick's love to surround her.

"Say something," he ordered as she continued to stare at him. "Kim. You don't have to take it if you don't want it. Hell, I just thought it was important for you to have something of your own—your own life." He swallowed. "Apart from me, I mean," he added as if the thought hurt him. He shifted restlessly on his injured leg, staring down at the lush carpet almost shyly. "I want you to know," he stated softly. "That I realize I can be pretty domineering—" His black eye scanned her face quickly. He hesitated. "I have to say this: I see you as a desirable woman, but as a person, too."

Kim's heart hurt, bursting with love for this passionate, impulsive man who faced her uncertainly. She felt torn between crying and throwing her arms around him. She knew instinctively that the gym was Nick's love gift. In offering it to her, he expected nothing. He only wanted to please her. "For me? No strings?"

"Damn right," he stated roughly, nearing her. He tilted his head down, examining her face. The pad of his thumb wiped away a tear near her eye and he swallowed. "Okay—I make mistakes. Big ones. I love you, woman. And I wanted to give you something that would please you. No ulterior motives. Got it?" He half smiled. "I can't tell if I've pleased you, or disappointed you," he whispered rawly.

Kim lifted her forefinger, tracing the grim line of his mouth. Nick was vulnerable to her, his tough-guy act covering honest and deep emotions. "I love you," he repeated stubbornly. "But I'm not trying to control you . . ."

"You're floundering, Nick," Kim whispered gently, full of her own deep emotions. Nick was the home she had searched for; he was all she would ever want or need. "It's a very nice present. Thank you."

He looked stunned. "You're accepting?"

"Didn't you think I would?" she asked, placing both her palms on his cheeks and drawing his face downward.

"I'm not in the doghouse?" His arms encircled her, drawing her against him. Then he grinned with all the Santos confidence. "Then tell me that you love me."

Kim traced the line of his lips with her tongue, following the broad planes of his shoulders with her palms. "Opportunist—"

His mouth sealed hers in a tender kiss.

Kim gave herself to the music, enjoying the freedom of the dance. It was June now, the third week since Nick's operation. She had expected him to be a bad patient, demanding and as contrary as a caged panther. Instead, Nick was a pussy cat, allowing her to help him in the painful therapeutic exercises. He'd sweated and groaned and cursed, his smile at her forced as a result of his pain—yet he was remarkably malleable.

"We're finally alone." His deep voice cut through the throbbing music. "I can't believe Duke packed the whole family off to Disneyland. Mom was almost as excited as Cherry. I have a feeling Duke will regret his charity."

"I want to watch you dance in the moonlight, honey," he said, turning off the light. His gaze flowed over her tight yellow T-shirt and black workout shorts, then down her bare legs to her feet. "You look like a fantasy."

Kim kept beat with the music, jogging in place. In the wall-sized mirror she watched him cross the midnight shadows of the workout room to a comfortable chair. He limped a little, padding across the polished wood in his bare feet. Bracing his hip and one hand on the chair arm, Nick leaned back against the paneling.

The moonlight crossing through the skylight touched the glossy black hair and flooded over his tall body. Dressed only in his cutoff jeans, Nick's tanned body blended with the shadows. The strong, lean lines of his torso and legs took Kim's breath away, heating her flesh despite the cool desert breeze wafting through the open window.

The music changed to a sensuous storm and Kim followed it. Swaying, lifting her arms into the shafts of moonlight, she neared his chair. Nick's eye glittered, following her movements. He looked desperately hungry for her, his hunger lodging deep inside her, weakening her legs.

The beat softly invaded the shadows as Kim danced, touching him lightly with the drift of her hand. He swallowed, his large hands gripping the arms of the chair, the muscles of his chest rigid as she spun away from him.

Nick's voice was raspy. "You're beautiful, Kim. You move like liquid silk."

She eased the rubber band from her ponytail, letting her unruly curls flow about her shoulders. Nick needed to pay: he'd been ruthless in his pursuit, challenging and maddening her, making her face the painful shadows of her life.

His dark skin—stretched tightly over thrusting facial bones—glistened in the silvery light. His grim mouth, bracketed by lines, was as formidable as the hard set of his clean-shaven jaw.

Sliding her fingers through her hair, Kim lifted its weight, her hips swaying with the music. The strands slowly filtered through her fingers and she *felt* Nick's inhaled breath, felt his heart race, throbbing to the sensual music.

"Damn! Do you have any idea what you're doing, woman?"

Kim smiled slowly. Oh, he'd pay for loving her. She didn't plan to make it easy for him. "Don't you like it, darling?"

He swallowed, his raw-boned features stark with desire. "I've been giving you time—"

She caught the lower edge of her tight T-shirt, raising it as her wide-spread legs flexed with the music's beat. Gyrating and thrusting her hips toward him sensuously, Kim stripped the T-shirt from her body. It floated through the shadows to Nick like a yellow flower on a June breeze.

His hand caught and crushed the garment. But his eye locked to Kim's full, swaying breasts. "If you're playing games, little girl . . . I'm not up to them yet."

"Threats, Nick?" Stalking rhythmically toward him, Kim stripped off her black shorts and briefs, discarding them with a sweeping, high leg lift.

Riveted to the graceful movements of her nude body, his gaze locked on the strength of her thighs and the triangular nest of his desire. "My God, Kim—"

Sensuously, Kim neared him. Easing her breasts against his hard chest, she felt white-hot electricity flow through her, sensitizing her nipples into hard erotic buds. Sliding gently against his chest, she luxuriated in the thrusting desire rising against her soft stomach.

"Do you need me, Nick?" she whispered, swaying, kissing the hard planes of his chest.

"Like I need air," he gasped. "You're making it very hard for me—"

"Hard?" Kim smiled up at him, running her palm down his stomach and over the contours of his cutoff jeans. She unsnapped his waistband, trailing her fingertips over his flat stomach. "Shy, darling? Don't be. I want you, too."

His thick eyebrows shot together. "This isn't funny, Kim. There's more at stake here than a fast—"

Kim bent to kiss his navel, then straightened to lock her arms about his neck. His fingers settled—trembling, lightly—on the bared curve of her waist. She stroked his chest with her softness, nuzzling the base of his neck with her nose. "You're an extremely desirable man, Nicholas A. Santos. *Accessible* Nick."

Peering up at his rigid face through the length of her lashes, she asked, "Do I have to tell you I love you to use your body?"

One eyebrow lifted, his hands tightening on her waist. With classic Nick Santos arrogance, he ordered, "If you mean it, lady, tell me, and I'll let you use the hell out of me."

Cradling the back of his head, Kim urged his mouth to hers. "It's a tall order, gambler man. It may take a long time."

His left hand stroked her body on an upward journey, filtering through her hair. Twisting a strand around his finger, Nick smiled at the contrast—her white-gold hair clinging to his tanned finger.

He stared into her eyes for a moment, then downward to her golden skin meshed with the tanned planes of his chest. "I was afraid I'd pushed you too hard, Kim. That I took what you didn't want to give . . ."

Stroking his newly shaven jaw, tracing along it and down his muscular neck, Kim savored the scents of the desert air mixing with Nick's lime after shave and the scent—so male—of his body. A blend of texture and colors and boy and man, Nick could be as savage as he could be gentle.

She unsnapped his jeans, sliding them from him with a sensuous brush of her palms. "I'd rather be with you, excited by you and alive, than in any portion of my previous life. You make my life then seem as desolate as the desert dryness beyond us, Nick," she whispered seriously. "If it weren't for you, I would have continued through life alone and cold. I feel as if I'm finally home now, darling."

Stroking his injured thigh lightly with her fingertips, Kim knelt to kiss the freshly healed scar. Gently, she tugged his wrist, guiding him down to the exercise mat. "I need you, Nick."

Holding himself from her, Nick's eye burned over her face. "Tell me you love me, damn you. Tell me."

She smiled, kissing his palm and leading it to her breast. "Make me, lover."

"Kim," he groaned, fighting his raging desire.

Instantly, her fingers feathered over his thigh and she frowned. "Are you hurting, darling?"

He grinned, feeling the heat wash over him. "I'm in agony. Heal me."

Gently, Kim pushed him back to the mat. Kneeling beside him, she trailed kisses from his shoulder to his ankle. Blazing now, Nick watched the moonlight swathe her lithe body, striking sparks off her silvery hair. Drawing her over him, he closed his eye as she settled softly against him.

"I love you, woman," he whispered as her mouth settled on his. "You're all I'll ever want."

Stroking her thigh, cupping the velvety softness of her hips with his palms, Nick thought he'd died as her moist heat accepted him.

"Am I hurting you?" she asked again as her teeth lightly nipped his earlobe. "Nick?"

Her lips were so sweet on his, tasting of hunger. Cupping the back of her head, Nick drank of her mouth, her tongue playing with his. She coiled about him urgently, clawing him nearer with her fingertips, her hips writhing and thrusting. "I need you, darling. I need you now."

He knew. She needed him to cleanse her and all that had happened before him. Purring, moaning, drawing him deeper within her, Kim fought her past and met her future. Out of her desperation rose a quivering, throbbing race for pleasure and for rebirth. Flying, soaring, meeting her demands, he knew she faced the old pains and raced toward the security of their love.

Cradling her, following her journey through the old wounds, Nick knew his time would come; that, for now, she needed the bare strength, the essence within him.

And he gave it. Then finally, she shot out of her pain, her whisper aching and full. "Nick."

Only then—with the softness of her about him, his heartbeat sounding in his ears—did Nick forget everything but the thrusting pleasure as they moved rapidly into a sensual golden haze.

Entering through the open window, the desert breeze smelled of sand and sagebrush as it cooled their intertwined bodies. Nick's heart slowed its race and Kim, dewy and soft, settled gently beside him, her thigh draped across his uninjured leg, the flat of her hand skimming the length of his body slowly.

"I'm sorry, Nick," she whispered raggedly against the damp planes of his shoulder. "I did use you."

He lifted the damp strands of hair tangled about her neck, stroking her softly. Tipping her chin upward, he kissed her gently. "That's what it's all about, honey. To be here for you. Always." Nick smiled. Kim was beautiful, lying sated in his arms. Shades of honey and gold and silver. Shadows of a woman's pleasure darkened her eyes and touched her lips. He traced her frown, loving the silkiness of her flesh, the heat of their love upon it. "What's wrong, lady mine?"

"Oh, my. How awful." Her voice was wispy, her expression confused. "How unlike—"

"A lady?" he supplied with a chuckle. "Gambling lady, you *are* my dream, my lover."

In the moonlit shadows he watched her mouth form the words. "I love you, Nick."

"I know you do, honey," he said with a touch of his old arrogance, drawing her closer. "The next time is for the both of us."

Holding him from her, Kim raised her lips, then averted her face almost shyly. "I have something for you, Nick."

He smoothed her soft breast, teasing the erect peak. "Mmm, I know."

Turning from him, she smiled over her shoulder. "I

wanted to do something for you, Nick. New and . . . unlike me . . . before you."

She took his finger and led it to the pale roundness of her hip. In the moonlight, he saw a tiny heart. Bending to better see it, Nick read the words—"I love you, Nick."

"Damn," he murmured as a tear trailed down his cheek, falling to the tiny heart, blurring the ink drawing.

"The tattoo isn't real, my love. But it's the thought that counts, my darling," Kim whispered, turning into his arms. "And I do love you, gambler man. With all my heart, for all my life."